The man came close behind her, his body a hair's from her tingling back. Helen's breathing became erratic, and then was cut off when she felt his fingers slipping between low-cut back of her dress and her blazing hot skin.

'The label was sticking out,' he said in a throaty voice.

'Oh,' she whispered.

His hands spanned her waist, and she looked into the mirror to see his expression. It didn't reassure her. The sultriness of his eyes had that come-to-bed look, and his mouth was definitely sensual.

'I'm ready,' she muttered, pulling against his hands.'

'So am I.' He didn't move, only held her imprisoned. 'More than ready.'

'Good,' she said, shifting her weight and pretending to stumble. Her stiletto heel ground down into his foot and she slid away when he reacted.

'Oh, dear,' she said, as his pained face caught her conscience. 'I didn't mean to hurt you!'

'You're supposed to pretend that was an accident, according to the usual rules,' he grated.

'I have my own rules,' she said grimly. 'Oughtn't we to leave?'

'If that's what you want.'

'That's what I want,' she said, convincing herself.

NO GENTLE LOVING

BY

SARA WOOD

MILLS & BOON LIMITED
ETON HOUSE   18-24 PARADISE ROAD
RICHMOND   SURREY   TW9 1SR

First published in Great Britain 1988
by Mills & Boon Limited

© Sara Wood 1988

Australian copyright 1988
Philippine copyright 1988
This edition 1988

ISBN 0 263 76120 7

Set in Baskerville 10 on 11 pt.
01 – 8810 – 56709

Typeset in Great Britain by JCL Graphics, Bristol

Made and printed in Great Britain

CHAPTER ONE

HELEN beamed happily at her departing guests. It had been a wonderful farewell party, with everyone acting as though she was going to be away for two years, rather than two months. She was lucky to have such affectionate friends.

'Have a lovely time, Helen!'

'Don't you dare swank your tan at me when you return!'

'Watch out for the natives!'

Her smile faltered a little. Then she was being turned around and hugged by her boss. Only he and her father—who was beginning to wash up by the sound of it—knew why she was really going.

'Bye, Helen.' John Fraser looked down on the tiny curvaceous blonde in his arms. 'I look forward to your notes and photographs. Spring in Crete is reputed to be fantastic: I envy you.'

'Bye, John,' she said gratefully. 'I'm sure it'll make a wonderful place for Flower Walks. You *are* an old opportunist, aren't you?' she continued in a teasing tone. 'I'm supposed to be on holiday. Still, I'll come back with lots of ideas, I'm sure.'

John laughed, making his face even more wrinkled than it was already. At sixty, having led an outdoor life planning safaris all over the world, the weather had taken a toll on his face, but left warmth in his big heart. He'd become a second father to Helen when she joined his specialist holiday agency seven years ago at the age of

eighteen. His enthusiastic guidance had turned her into
one of his top researchers. For the last two years she had
been creating guided walks in France to follow her highly
successful Flower Walks in Madeira. When she told him
that she had to go to Crete as soon as possible, and why,
he had immediately given her two months' leave. And
just as immediately asked whether she would just 'have a
little look around' while she was there!

In fact, it was a heaven-sent blessing to Helen, to be
able to tell her friends that she was researching new walks.
She couldn't yet bring herself to explain the real reason. It
was important that she came to terms with her past before
she let the truth be known.

'Dad? You leave those dishes!' she called out, hurrying
into the kitchen. 'Now didn't I tell you . . .'

The big, blond man in the wheelchair grinned at his
daughter in affection. 'You're tired, pet.' Dick Summers
continued to dunk plates at an alarming rate. 'You have a
big day ahead of you tomorrow. Go to bed, I'll clean up.'

'You old martyr,' she grumbled. 'You just want to tell
your cronies what an unchauvinistic——'

'If you're going to stand there gassing, grab a tea-towel
and use up a bit of your energy on those plates,' he said
calmly.

With a suppressed smile, she did so. He washed the
dirty dishes with an efficiency born from years of practice,
and she automatically dried them. They'd worked as a
team for a long time. Her mother, Liz, would cook the
meals; she and her father cleared up afterwards, loving
the ritual. There had been more time lately to be together,
thought Helen wistfully, since her mother had died three
months ago. Her hands slowed.

'You've been holding that plate for seventy-two and a
half seconds,' said her father. 'Fallen in love with it, have
you?'

'Don't be silly.' Helen didn't respond with her usual disarming grin. She decided to voice her fears. 'I—I'm not sure I want to go, Dad.'

He groaned. 'You have to! I've arranged all night poker games while you're away! You can't let my mates down now; they've bought the beer and peanuts, and the neighbours have laid on a rota of beautiful maidens to prop our eyelids open with matchsticks.'

Her laugh was unsteady. Dick shot her a look and shook the suds from his hand, seeing that her worries were serious. 'Come and talk, pet,' he said gently, setting the electric chair in motion.

She followed him into the sitting-room and curled up on the floor with her head on his lap. As usual, he said nothing, waiting for her to begin. Dick Summers was renowned for his ability to listen to everyone's troubles.

'It's difficult to explain exactly what I feel. But inside me,' she said slowly, trying to make sense of her confused emotions, 'there's a kind of restlessness. I feel half-empty, unfinished. I know that I won't be settled until I have been to Crete and learnt something about the people and . . .' Her voice tailed away and her father smoothed her golden head in understanding. 'But I'm afraid to go. I don't know the language—it even *looks* odd with those weird-shaped letters—and it will be very strange. I don't want it to be strange. What if I hate it? How will I feel then?'

'You'll come home to me. I'll be here, waiting for you. And all your friends, especially those young men who kept trying to whisk you into the kitchen alone, when I wasn't looking.'

Helen gave a wry smile and lifted her head to look at him. 'They're nice, but they're not important. You are. So long as I have you batting on my side, I'll be OK. Will you write to me? I'll get a poste-restante address in Agios

Nikolaos and send you a postcard the minute I arrive.'

'Sure. I'll write and tell you how the poker game is going. Send me a pack of matches from the posh hotels you dine in every night.'

She laughed. 'Oh, sure. On my savings?'

The Summers family had found it hard to scrape a living. Dick had suffered an accident on a building site very early on in his marriage which had paralysed him, and since then his wife Liz had shouldered the burden as breadwinner. Helen had ploughed her money into the family kitty when she'd started work, and only by limiting her spending to essentials had she managed to save a little.

'I've got something put by,' said her father awkwardly, pressing some notes into her hand. 'I know it'll be hard for you, trying to fit in, and if you get depressed, or if you want to celebrate, I'd like you to take yourself to a grand hotel and a have a slap-up meal. Will you do that for me?'

'Dad, I——' Now she knew why he had stopped making his Saturday night visits to the local club: he'd given up the highlight of his week to offer her his idea of a good time. 'I'd love that,' she said, sniffing a little. 'It's a wonderful idea, thanks.'

He pretended to endure her hug with heavy sighs. 'I'll want to hear all about it,' he said. 'What you wore, and tales about the other diners—make some up if they're all boring!'

'I'll do that,' she promised, pushing away her dislike of eating alone in public.

He ruffled her abundant hair, and they continued clearing away the debris of the party. But Dick Summers couldn't help glancing frequently at his beautiful daughter. He wanted to remember every bit of her: the loose, flowing, corn-gold hair, with the little quiff in the front like his; the soft, flawless bloom of her skin; her tiny face with its sensual lips, so like her mother's. Dick almost dropped a heavy ash-tray as the bolt of memory shot through him.

Apart from her fair hair, Helen was like her mother in every way. She had the same dark, velvet eyes that could melt a man with a look, the neat little nose that crinkled when she laughed, the sudden, joyous smile infecting everyone around. And, he had to admit, Helen might be tiny, but she had some spectacular curves that drew the men from miles around.

In a way, he hoped she didn't like Crete. It was selfish, he knew, but then he wanted her to come home to him. Both of them had never said what lay in their minds: that there was the possibility she might never return.

Helen lay awake for a long time that night. Her rucksack was packed, her alarm was set, the taxi booked. And she was afraid.

It had been only a few days after her mother Liz had died that she'd been told the most devastating news of her life.

When he was on holiday in Crete as a young man, her father had become friendly with a young girl called Maria Zakro, who worked in a taverna. In fact, for Dick, the holiday romance was serious: he loved Maria. Under the moonlit sky, beside the Aegean sea one night, they had made love. Yet something held Maria in Crete; she wouldn't follow him to England when he returned, and, though they corresponded and he declared his love, she always gently explained that she could never leave her homeland.

Helen bit her lip as she remembered her father's face when he'd told the story. It had held a distant, far-away look, softened by love. One day, apparently, Maria had turned up out of the blue, arriving at his tiny terraced house to ask for his help. She was pregnant with his child.

Dick had gripped Helen's shoulders hard at that moment. 'You are that child, pet. You are Maria's child. My love child.' As she stared at him, reluctant to comprehend, he gave her a little shake. 'Liz wasn't your mother.'

'What . . . what happened to Maria, then?' she asked in an unnaturally high voice. Her throat was dry as a bone and her hands had begun to shake. Liz had cuddled her, bathed her grazed knees, packed her school sandwiches, taken her to buy her first party dress . . .

'She came to live with me—you know my parents and I had gone our separate ways by then. It was in this very house that she died, Helen. After you were born. A fever, they said. But I always thought it was pining for her home. She missed the countryside and the wild flowers, and hated the dull greyness of our winter.

'Were you married?'

'No. I wish we had been. She refused marriage, and I knew that I couldn't imprison her here. One day she wanted to go home, you see. At first, to help me out after she had died, Liz and her mum next door cared for you while I worked on the building site, and then—well, I became fond of Liz and we married. Not long afterwards, I had the accident with that excavator and wasn't able to walk again. Nor could I father any more children, Helen,' he said gently.

She looked at him with sympathy and despair. 'I didn't know! Mum—Liz——'

'That's why I didn't tell you, ' he said. 'You must forgive me, but she loved us both and couldn't bear the idea of you going off to find your roots. You were her child, to all intents and purposes. We even forgot you weren't, sometimes. I'd smashed all her chances of becoming a real mother, Helen. I couldn't take you away from her, too. It thrilled her when you called her Mum. She was very proud of you.'

'But my passport . . .'

'I filled in your application, remember? You were working so hard for John Fraser that it wasn't difficult for me to persuade you to let me handle it. You trusted me. You just signed your name.'

'Yes, I remember,' she said, a little bewildered that her father could be at all devious. He must have felt strongly about keeping her origins a secret. Dick had said he'd get her birth certificate from the bank and post her application form for her. When her passport had arrived, he'd slipped the certificate out of her hand and said he'd put it safely away. At the time, she'd been so thrilled at the thought of her first job abroad for John's company that she hadn't even noticed.

'How long would you have kept me in the dark, if Liz hadn't died?' she asked.

'I don't know,' he confessed. 'My conscience was nagging me. I think I would have told you soon. Please forgive me,' he begged.

Of course she had. Despite the shock of finding she was the product of an unknown culture, and that she felt suddenly alien and different, she understood completely. She believed Liz and her father had done the best for her. They had given her an enormously happy life so far, and she would be ever grateful for the noise and laughter that filled the house, with friends and neighbours always welcome.

Helen glanced at the clock. Two-thirty in the morning! Would she never sleep? She watched the hands creep round and then tried to clear her mind. When she arrived on the island, she wanted to feel alert. If she could sleep soon, and catch a nap on the plane, she'd be all right. The events of the last months receded and she began to relax at last.

Quietly, the manservant crossed the vast marble floor, his
footsteps silenced by the soft soles that his master insisted
on. Since his second heart attack, when he'd relinquished
control of his luxury hotel chain in favour of his son
Dimitri, Stavros had become unreasonably bad-
tempered. This evening was no exception.

'I don't see why I can't take over temporarily while
Dimitri's on holiday,' he growled to his wife. He took a
glass of Kir Royale from his servant and glared over the
top of it.

Agnes Kastelli sipped her Perrier water with a frosty
expression. 'The doctor said you weren't to work again.
For years I've been looking forward to your retire-
ment . . .'

'Damn it!' roared Stavros. 'I don't want to retire! I
could just keep an eye on the business . . .'

'*No, father!*'

Agnes and Stavros started at the vehement tones
coming from the huge patio windows, and turned to see
Dimitri, framed against the vast, snow-capped
mountains. He strode in quickly, lithe, youthful and
supple, irritating his father with the glow of health that
surrounded him. All his movements were fluid and feral,
the strongly corded muscles of his body showing that he
was a man who kept himself fit and denied himself the
excesses of life. This made him stand out in the world he
moved in; the indulgent, plump and powerful men who
were his competitors, associates and clients respected him
and admired the rigour that set him apart. But they found
his quiet assessment unnerving, the way he listened and
watched with those steady black eyes which seemed to
penetrate the lies, the bluster, the assumed confidence,
and strip the layers of people to arrive at the naked core

He didn't try to be liked, and that was unusual. Dimitri
Kastelli was a man who walked on mountain tops alone.

No amount of elegant suiting or hours chairing meetings
in boardrooms could conceal the fact that he came from
tough, proud Cretan stock. There was a suggestion of fire
beneath his façade. Wherever he travelled in the world,
masterminding every facet of the great Kastelli hotel chain,
he could command instant attention with an authority born
from inner strength. No one knew at what cost he had
earned that superb self-control. Discipline now came easily
to Dimitri. Ever since he could remember, he had choked
back any feelings of affection for his parents, recognising
that neither of them included him in their lives. His mother
lived on her nerves, petrified that his father would have an
affair or leave her. She had sent Dimitri to school in Athens
at an early age to ensure his father lavished all his spare
love on her. The ploy had failed: Stavros had no love for his
family. He lived for the business—it was almost food and
drink to him. There was no room left for a silent, lonely
boy.

And now Stavros didn't even have that one love any
more. It must be terrible, thought Dimitri, as he kissed
his mother's cold cheek dutifully, to be unable to fill your
days with work. He managed a sympathetic smile in his
father's direction, but was shaken by the venomous look
he received in response.

'I could take over. I'm not decrepit yet,' bellowed
Stavros.

'So I hear,' said Dimitri drily in a quiet voice. His
father's roar could have been heard in the valley below.
'But I'm seeing how my deputies manage without me.
It'll do them good to be at the sharp end for a while. And
you can't deny I deserve a holiday after four years of solid
work. You may not have noticed, but I've ony taken a
short break each Christmas and Easter. Besides, I still

have a couple of problems I want to take care of myself.'

'Oh? Tell me,' ordered Stavros sullenly. He hated being idle while his son controlled everything with such indecent skill. But then, Dimitri had never really been a child. He'd been an adult since the age of two.

Dimitri settled his long limbs in a huge chair which faced the cascading bougainvillaea on the terrace outside. He sipped his Kir slowly.

'I'm afraid I'm having to step up security,' he said casually. 'The President and the Prime Minister have both received threats to their lives, and naturally I'll increase checks at the hotels they'll be using over the Easter period and run extra investigations on the staff.'

'We didn't make all this fuss when my father owned the hotels,' observed his mother sharply.

Dimitri was silent. It was a sore point with her that she'd discovered Stavros had married her for ambition and not love, and that in accordance with Cretan custom her property was transferred to her husband. Yet she couldn't fault the way he had built up the chain and made the hotels the most prestigious and the safest in the world. The royal, the rich and the famous chose to stay in Kastelli-run hotels, knowing that neither the press nor scroungers could bother them and that there was no risk of abduction or injury during their stay in the impregnable buildings.

'I think I'll put a barrier and a guard on the road up to our valley,' he murmured. 'Just to keep out any stray hikers. You remember how we had the scare last year, when that idiot camper set the gorge ablaze.'

'Are you afraid of something?' asked his father shrewdly.

Dimitri hesitated, eyeing him speculatively. 'No. But I think we, too, are high-profile targets. Through us, any determined terrorist could reach any head of state he wanted.'

'That's far-fetched!' snorted his mother.

He lowered his black lashes over his eyes. He had no intention of telling her of the threats he'd personally received.

'It's about time we had a decent road, instead of that awful rough track,' continued Agnes. 'I'm getting too old to be bounced around like a sack of potatoes. The helicopter isn't always available, particularly since you've taken to using it when heads of state fly in to visit you.'

Dimitri steadily surveyed his mother. She must be over seventy now, and looked it. Wealth had once lent her an elegance through good grooming and *couture* clothes, but age and bitterness had finally caught up with her. He shivered, seeing in her face a vision of himself, alone and loveless as an old man.

'The road at this end must be repaired first,' he answered curtly. 'The men can't be everywhere at once.'

'Nor can a guard watch more than the road itself. Fence the whole valley in at its mouth,' she said. 'It belongs to us, after all.'

'Not all of it,' he reminded her, ignoring his father's indrawn breath. There would be a row if he didn't divert his mother.

'That Maria Zakro!' she grated, her face ugly.

Dimitri saw his father wince and his hands grip the sides of his chair, and spoke quietly to lower the tension.

'Legally, Mother, Maria owns that house and the two fields, as well as the right of way up to the high pastures. I can't fence in the whole valley, and well you know it.'

'She'll never come back!' she muttered. 'Not while I'm here! I won't allow it!'

'You can't stop her, it's her home,' snapped Stavros. 'And you'd better know, both of you, that I altered my will. When I die, half the estate goes to Maria and her child.'

Dimitri blanched. Only his father's high colour and feverish eyes prevented him from venting his hurt anger. He glanced at his mother and quickly strode to the tray of drinks, pouring champagne into cassis and making the shaking woman down it in one gulp.

'Your money and your property are yours to do with as you like, Father,' he said, carefully controlling his voice. 'But if you don't find Maria Zakro, you will have tied up half of Kastelli assets, and fifty per cent of the operation will grind to a halt. We can't survive under those circumstances.'

'I intend to find her,' he rasped. 'In fact, I think she *is* coming home. Why else should the bank's agent write to say that the lease on her place was not to be renewed? All these years, I've made sure her house has been kept in perfect order, ready for her return. And when she does arrive, I will welcome her, and her son or daughter!'

Dimitri winced. The manservant announced dinner and helped his father to the dining-room. Dimitri exchanged glances with his mother, the same unspoken anger and fear vibrating between them. Whatever their differences, they were agreed on this: if ever Maria Zakro should return, their lives would be an instant hell. The situation that had soured all their relationships would be opened up like an old wound. Half of the Kastelli empire would be handed on a plate to a woman they had come to hate and resent.

He squared his shoulders in determination, and Agnes released a little of her breath. When Dimitri set his mind on something, he always got it. No one had ever prevented him from his single-minded pursuit of his goals. If—when—Maria turned up, he would ensure that the business would not fall into her greedy hands. He'd worked too hard for too long to be thwarted and ousted from sole command.

During dinner he was grimly silent. There was nothing in his life except his work. It brought him alive and made his adrenalin run. His eyes glittered dangerously as the hatred swelled within him, and he concentrated on ways of ensuring that Maria Zakro and her child did not benefit from his father's generous hand.

CHAPTER TWO

HELEN had been walking for about forty minutes, and no vehicle had been along the road at all. Gloomily she dug into her pocket and drew out the chocolate bar that had been given to her by the couple who'd picked her up just outside Iraklion airport. That had been a good lift—all the way to Agios Nikolaos. She'd had lunch, sent some postcards, fixed up her poste-restante box and eventually hitched a ride with an enthusiastic American woman who was intending to visit the Minoan town of Gournia. Since then, nothing.

That wouldn't have been so bad in itself, since she enjoyed walking, but she was travelling towards the blackest storm clouds she'd ever seen! A few large spots of rain began to splash on her face, and she hurried over to shelter for a moment beneath the branches of a mimosa tree which was heavily laden with fragrant yellow blossom. Her thin, baggy stormcoat was in the front pocket of her rucksack and was easily extracted.

With every stride Helen took towards her mother's village her steps became more hesitant. Not only had it been cloudy since she'd arrived, but there was a chilly wind, too, that was nipping at her earlobes. Walking had made her warm, of course, and she'd discarded her blue sweater, so she wore only a pale T-shirt and shorts. Nevertheless, she'd been expecting sunshine, and found the prospect of arriving in a strange house in bad weather surprisingly daunting. Perhaps, she thought, she was more worried about her own reaction to Crete and its people than she realised.

The gentle clopping sound of hooves penetrated her reverie, and she turned around to see an old man riding on a donkey.

'*Kalimera,*' she called politely.

'*Kalimera,*' he grinned.

'Vronda?' Helen pointed in what she thought was the turn-off to the valley and the man nodded, indicating that she was nearly there.

The donkey plodded slowly by and she was alone again in the vast landscape. The rain began to fall hard, as straight as icy arrows from heaven. Helen tucked her long plait into her collar and drew the ties of her hood firmly around her small face.

'Keep going, I'm relying on you,' she said with a sigh, looking down at her size fours in the sturdy walking-boots. 'Only a few more miles to go.'

There was a turning where she expected it to be, but no road sign saying that was the way to Vronda—and the track really didn't look fit for vehicles. Surely this couldn't lead to the village! She decided there must be another road, a little further on. She checked her map. No, she'd been right, for there, directly ahead, was the gash in the mountains which indicated the Vronda gorge.

'Not a very promising sight,' she muttered to herself, eyeing the uneven road ahead. 'It looks as though I'm about to step back in time a few hundred years. How primitive is this place, I wonder?'

The great sweep of misty mountains and the utter silence—apart from the falling rain—gave the landscape an eerie feeling to it and made her feel even lonelier. Helen began to wish she was somewhere else—anywhere would do. The trouble was that her expectations had been high. After all, Maria had told her father that Vronda was a fertile valley and the village was thriving. She sighed.

That was a long time ago now.

Apparently Maria had not found it difficult to rent out her house and land when she'd gone to stay in the town of Agios Nikolaos. Rent had been paid to the village priest, who had sent the money to her bank. When Maria had travelled to England, the National Bank of Greece had transferred the account, thus keeping her whereabouts a secret from the villagers—presumably to avoid scandal.

No one knew of Maria's pregnancy, and Helen had promised her father that she would go very carefully at first, in case the people were scandalised and refused to welcome her.

When Maria had died, all her possessions had been left to Dick. He'd been ashamed that he had done little else with Maria's property, apart from making a periodical check on the income from the rent. In fact, the house had continued to earn rent until Dick had cancelled the lease shortly after Liz had died, knowing that it was time Helen knew the truth. Somehow Helen had gained the impression that she was on her way to a pleasant little whitewashed cottage surrounded by olive groves.

That impression was fading fast. All the indications now were that few people travelled up this road or had the money to repair the pot-holes—and that meant limited prosperity. The cottage could be in a state of total disrepair!

And yet someone in these parts had money: that was a helicopter, flying low ahead. Helen narrowed her eyes against the icy wind that was beginning to blow from the snow-capped mountains in the far distance. The helicopter seemed to be seeking the shelter of the valley. It disappeared and reappeared from behind the hills, and then was swallowed up by the gorge itself.

Because of the lowering sky, the light was fading, even though it was only four o'clock. As she climbed the steep, zigzagging track, her boots slipped on the huge wet stones and she had to pick her way very carefully. It was one of the paved roads laid by the Turks: a *kalderim*. The dark red earth holding the stones began to flow like a thick, muddy wine as the rain became torrential. She was quite high up now, but still in a fertile valley of olive trees between hills covered in sage and thyme. Carpets of yellow-horned poppies and purple vetch mingled with white turban buttercups under the trees: it must be a wonderful sight in the sun, she mused.

Sun! It wouldn't rain for ever. She'd feel more cheerful in a day or so. Meanwhile . . .

Helen whirled around, her spirits revived. There was the unmistakable sound of a car, driving far too fast surely, for the twisting, uneven narrow track. But she'd be more than willing to risk putting her life in the driver's hands, just to get to the cottage faster, to dig out a packet of warming beef curry from her rucksack and make herself cosy!

There was no doubting that the driver would be bound for Vronda; this road didn't lead anywhere else. On her father's old map, the road came to a dead end at the beginning of the gorge. She was certain to be offered a lift in this filthy weather, because she'd heard that Cretans were incredibly generous. That had been her experience even in the few short hours she'd been on the island, too. One greengrocer had pushed two extra oranges into her rucksack after she had sniffed the two she'd bought and beamed at their fragrant aroma. The woman at the post office had even offered Helen a room for the night—as a non-paying guest—till the threatened storm had passed.

Happily, thinking of impending comfort, Helen positioned herself on a bend and faced downhill, the rain lashing at her freezing legs. She caught glimpses of the

shiny red pick-up truck as it expertly negotiated the pot-
holes and swerved to avoid the subsidence at the edge of
the track. Here and there, where torrents of rich brown
sediment poured down the hillside, the track was awash
with cascades of water. It took some nerve to drive up
here, in these conditions, she thought, even if you were
used to terrible roads.

The truck crested a small rise and she waved madly.
The driver, somewhere behind the manic windscreen
wipers, made no sign, but the truck began to slow and
Helen slid off her rucksack, so that she would be ready to
jump in the minute he stopped.

But as she peered with difficulty through the streaming
window, she saw that the darkly tanned face was glaring
at her beaming, happy face, and wasn't smiling or
friendly at all. The satanic Cretan, with the classical
Greek nose and carved, disapproving lips was actually
shooting her a look of glowering suspicion!

Her smile faltered for a moment before she was able to
force her lips into a curve again, but as she leaned
forwards to speak to the driver—expecting him to wind
the window down at least—his mouth compressed and the
truck shot away half drenching her as it hit a sheet of
water!

'You callous swine!' she yelled, at this, the last straw.
'You mean-minded, ignorant, evil-hearted pig! Arrogant, selfish, ill-mannered *dog!*' she screamed into the
wind, hoping vehemently that Handsome Harry was
looking in the rear-view mirror at her small, raging
figure.

The truck disappeared. She looked down at her mud-
splattered legs and didn't know whether to explode with
fury again or cry. Helen fought bravely with her
emotions. For a long time she'd held back her grief at
Liz's death, helping her father to weather his own sorrow.

Then had come the shock of learning she had Greek blood in her veins and a stranger for a mother. All her muddled feelings of grief, uncertainty and an uncharacteristic pessimism welled up within her. The miserable weather and that heartless driver made her feel worse. He'd been really thoughtless! Of all the . . . Helen's fists clenched, and she forgot everything else but her anger.

She strode on uphill, planning foul revenge when she met the man in the village. He'd be sorry he acted with such a lack of chivalry, even if he didn't understand a word she was saying when she tore strips off him! Small she might be, but huge men had quailed at her scorn before. Her temper wasn't often roused, but woe betide anyone in her way when it was!

She turned a tight bend. As she had expected, the Vronda valley lay ahead, stretching between a range of hills. She couldn't see the village, or Maria's cottage which was opposite it, because the valley meandered considerably, but she knew that the gentle gradient of the track would take her there soon. What she hadn't expected, however, was the sight of a red and white pole across the road and a small guard hut beside it.

'Now, why would that be there?' she wondered aloud. 'A police check? Or some kind of welcoming committee?' In fact, it looked like a border control, that impression gaining possibility when she saw that the hut was manned by someone in some kind of uniform. His peaked cap could occasionally be seen every time he thrust his head out of the hut window to look down the road in her direction. Putting on a pleasant smile, she walked up to the hut, under close scrutiny from the man.

'Hello, *kalimera*,' she said cheerfully.

The middle-aged, thick-set man looked at her very suspiciously without any answering smile or greeting.

'Road bad. Go back.'

She frowned, a little surprised, both at the lack of charm and the remark. The road ahead couldn't be any worse than the one she'd come on. This part of it followed the valley floor and therefore must be more protected. She smiled brilliantly.

'I'm a good walker.' She waggled her little boots at him and patted her rucksack. 'I can climb mountains.' Her hands described acutely pointed triangles and her knees lifted to mimic climbing. She tried hard not to giggle, thinking that she sounded rather like a well-rehearsed foreign entrant in the Miss World competition.

'Road bad,' said the man doggedly.

She looked down the valley. 'I can walk on the fields,' she added brightly, realising that there was no need for her to keep on the track at all. It couldn't hurt, surely, if she made her way through the olive groves? What on earth was the man babbling about?

'No. Kastelli fields.' He barred her way with a short, powerful arm.

He hadn't responded to her charm at all, and that surprised her. She was used to men throwing themselves at her feet, and although she found that rather unappealing and had always longed to meet a man who was less slave-like than her band of admirers, it did come as a shock to find someone so immune! Then she remembered, with an inner grin of self-mockery at her own conceit, that she looked ludicrous at the moment. All he could see was a midget in a baggy anorak that covered everything except a little face and brown shins, and feet in sensible socks and unsexy boots! A man stranded on a desert island for ten years would hesitate before chatting her up!

Nevertheless, she smiled sweetly, thinking that she ought to let him know she wasn't just a casual hiker, but knew where she was going.

'I go to Vronda,' she said firmly. 'I sleep Vronda.'

What else could she say? The man's thick accent and
limited vocabulary meant she couldn't explain or
elaborate much.

'Road closed. Broken bad. Danger. No way to Vronda.
Is . . .' he seemed to be searching for some words in his
memory '. . . i-so-la-ted. Un-rea-cha-ble.'

Now where, she wondered, did he get those particular
words from? They sounded like someone else's
vocabulary and someone else's pronounciation. That
reminded her: the truck! Something fishy was going on.
She narrowed her eyes. She didn't like people trying to
make a fool of her.

'A car came up this road,' she said, a note of steel in her
voice. 'Car go to Vronda, I go to Vronda.'

The man bit his lip, evidently worried. Got you! she
exulted, letting her triumph show in her eyes.

'Private,' he said stubbornly, waving his arm at the
whole valley. 'Is Mr Kastelli.'

Not all of it, she thought. One chunk of it is mine. 'You
Vronda man?' she asked. He nodded, and she decided to
mention her mother's name. He was about fifty-five and
might remember her. So, hoping he could read maps, she
pulled it out, deciding not to tell him who she was until
she felt more secure and welcome. This she had decided
long before she left home. It made sense to do as her
father had suggested, and see how everyone reacted to her
first. She jabbed the map with her finger, pointing to her
house. 'This not private,' she said. 'Not Mr Kastelli. I go
here. House of Maria Zakro.'

The man froze. Helen looked up in alarm. Had they all
condemned her mother for leaving? Did anyone around
here know she had been pregnant and unmarried, too?

'Zakro?' he said stupidly.

'Yes,' she said with an unaccustomed sharpness. She
was tired, hungry, cold and wet, and standing in the

pouring rain wasn't helping her temper. 'I have a key.'
She pantomimed unlocking a door and sleeping.

'Wait,' he said, withdrawing into the hut and reaching
for a telephone. His voice sounded excited.

Now what? she thought gloomily, stuffing her hands
into her pockets. If her father had cancelled the lease,
whoever had been living there and working the land
should have left last month. Unless . . . She groaned.
Perhaps they were still there. She might arrive to find it
inhabited by a huge family, and there would be nowhere
for her to sleep! The thought made her almost weep with
frustration.

'Wait,' said the man again, drawing the peak of his cap
over his eyes as he stuck his head out of the little hut
window. 'Mr Kastelli come.'

Lightning snaked across the sky, making her jump.
The big landowner. He might speak English and she
could explain. Then she heard the sound of a truck
reversing along the road ahead and her face fell as she put
a couple of facts together. Mr Kastelli must be handsome
Harry in the snazzy new pick-up, who'd brutally ignored
her earlier! She wouldn't get much help from *him*.

Her small shoulders rose, and the voluptuous mouth
thinned. Ah, well, every cloud had a silver lining. This
would be her opportunity to vent her anger: she was
spoiling for a fight. Anyone who drove past a soaking wet
hiker going along the same remote road was an out and
out pig, and she intended to make sure that he knew what
she thought of him.

The truck backed up to the barrier, and Helen expected
the man to jump out and approach her, but he sat
waiting, and she could just see his fingers impatiently
drumming on the wheel. Helen's dark eyes flashed
dangerously. Just because he owned vast tracts of land
didn't give him the right to treat her like a servant! She'd

be blowed if she'd go running to him.

The uniformed guard gave her a small push and she rounded furiously on him.

'Leave me alone!' she cried, planting her hands on her hips and withering him with a glare. Lightning and thunder split the air in unison, and suddenly huge hailstones began to beat down, bouncing on the ground and turning it white in seconds. 'Oh, hell,' she muttered, driving for shelter under the overhanging roof of the hut.

After a moment, the truck door opened and a pair of long, black-booted legs swung out. She was amazed that the man hadn't waited for the hailstorm to end, but then he'd seemed to be in a tearing hurry earlier. Perhaps he had slaves waiting to be beaten, she thought sourly. Her cynical eyes travelled, with as much insolence as she could muster, up the tight black leather trousers. Warning bells sounded in her head as she saw that these weren't the legs and thighs of an ordinary man at all: those hips were too lean and sexy, and the waist too narrow. She flicked a rapidly alerted glance over the big black leather jacket, its softness evident from the way it hung in easy folds, and the dull thud of the hailstones as they drummed into the man's body.

Still angry, her chin defiantly tilted, she lifted mocking eyes to his and was immediately transfixed.

He stood in the icy, lashing gale, his head unprotected. And yet in all that maelstrom there was a profound still-ness about him, a silent, watching aura, that magically dispelled the wildness of the elements and created an oasis of calm as he confronted her: immovable like the far mountains, as deep and inpenetrable as a black mountain lake. To Helen, it seemed that the very impassivity which held her spellbound hid not a dull, stolid man, but one who was slowly absorbing every aspect of her, quietly analysing her strengths and weaknesses, and filing away the information for future use. It was an incredibly unnerving experience, especially as she felt an odd frisson of excitement under his steady gaze. For his straddled legs and brooding face somehow made her startlingly aware of a blatant sexuality which was so strong that it made Helen suddenly nervous of being a woman, and thankful that she would not interest this predatory male.

He neither acknowledged her with a nod or a smile, nor seemed aware of the weather. He held his proud, dark head high, so that Helen's view was one of his angled jaw and sharp cheekbones, mercilessly pounded by the relentless hail. Her impression was that of a man who was unaffected by the vagaries of life, but drove his way directly to his goals. She was fascinated.

'You have lost your way,' he said in pefect English, the low, velvety voice shocking her with its richness. He spoke from somewhere deep in that big chest, she thought, the words resonating in the cavities behind his ribs. Her large brown eyes had widened and were fixed on him solemnly. He stepped closer so that she could hear him above the noise of the wind.

Helen automatically drew back. 'No, I haven't,' she said firmly, trying not to be intimidated. He dominated even the landscape, the dramatic cleft of the gorge behind him a fitting setting. That vibrant, almost tangible stillness of his would hold an audience in thrall more surely than a merely aggressive approach. And the raw animal sensuality of his nature must disconcert women and threaten men.

'You want Vronda, I believe.' He checked his watch and frowned, apparently wishing he was somewhere else. 'That is in the next valley.'

How could he sound helpful and charming and utterly dangerous? 'No, it's not.' If she knew anything, she knew how to use a map and orientate herself—she'd been doing it for years.

Kastelli's black eyes glittered. 'You are a stranger to Crete? When did you arrive?'

'I am a stranger and I arrived this morning,' she said, her teeth beginning to chatter. She hated getting warm walking and then having to stop and get cold again. 'Look, my muscles are going to seize up if I don't start moving again.'

Thick black lashes, sparkling with water, swooped down on to his cheekbones as he quietly surveyed her bare legs. 'You could jump up and down,' he suggested with a mocking glance.

And you, thought Helen grimly, could go jump in a lake. 'Well,' she said with a big smile, deciding to bluff it out, 'this *has* been nice. But I must move on now.'

'You would waste your time. I live here. I know. There's nothing up here, only my land. You have made a mistake.'

'Look,' she said, as if addressing a child, 'you and your pet watchdog here are up to something odd, and I know it. He says the road is closed, yet he let you through in a truck. If it's safe for you, it's safe for me. I am an expert map-reader and know that this is the right valley, so let's stop playing bureaucratic games. You're getting soaking wet, I'm eager to get to my destination. It seems a good idea to call a halt to this chat. You might even consider giving me a lift.'

There was a long silence as Kastelli studied her. 'Where did you say you were going?' he murmured silkily, his eyes watchful.

'Maria Zakro's house.'

There was a noticeable swell in his chest, and Helen looked at him curiously. His mouth had tightened considerably and held a sneer of distaste.

'What for?'

'Shelter. You might enjoy the masochism of getting cold and wet, but I don't. Can we have the inquisition somewhere else?' she asked sarcastically.

'I said, what for?' he barked, grabbing her arm.

Helen shook herself free, incredibly angry at his autocratic manner. It hadn't taken long for the charm to be wiped off his haughty face.

'My, my,' she said coldly. 'You do get excited easily, don't you? I'm staying there, not that it's any business of yours.'

Every muscle, every one of his sinews had tensed. Helen didn't like the hostile signals she was getting. It seemed that people around here weren't exactly sympathetic to her mother. Unless, of course, he'd done something illegal to the property and was trying to avoid discovery.

'You know Maria? She is a friend of yours?' he asked softly, a terrible stillness in his body.

'No.' Her lip trembled slightly. Damn him!

He let out a breath quietly, its warmth misting the air in front of him. 'You're renting the place from her? As a little holiday home?'

Patronising man! So, he was fishing for information, was he? Helen found a particular pleasure in not giving him much.

'I'm on holiday, yes.'

His dark brows knitted together. 'You seem well fitted out for walking.'

'Yes.'

Helen was becoming sullen now, knowing that he would stand there and question her until he was satisfied, and that there wasn't much she could do about it except protest. Despite the air of repose and contemplation that he projected, it was evident from the alertness of his eyes and the way he stood that he was ready to move with light-

ning speed should she decide to try to escape his barrage
of questions by setting off along the road.

'You're not intending to walk in the hills?'

'Yes, I am.' She was even more pleased to find that this
annoyed him.

'That's not wise. The roads are dangerous. When my
guard said the road was closed, he thought you were
going to the end of the gorge where there have been
landslides. It's not safe to walk any further than the end of
the valley. You must not go into the gorge itself.'

He seemed infuriated that she made no answer, but
merely stared at him levelly. Kastelli was obviously a man
who regarded the whole valley as his own and resented
anyone who entered it. How arrogant! She'd make sure
she used every one of Maria's rights of way just to make a
point!

He moved closer, still effectively barring her exit, his
black-clad body trembling with the effort he was making
to control his temper. The hail had turned into rain now
and drenched his bare head, making the thick black curls
glisten with a thousand droplets which clustered in the
tangles till the wind whipped them away.

'I'm afraid you have come here for nothing. Maria has
cheated you,' he said in a tight, hard voice. 'The house is
almost ruined. You can't stay there in this terrible
weather. I'll see what I can do to help you. Wait a
minute.'

He returned to the truck and started talking, puzzling
Helen until she realised that he must be using a car
telephone. That was how the guard had contacted him, of
course. She slumped miserably against the wall, chewing
over what he had said. Nothing was going right! It had
been too much to expect that the place would be in a
reasonable condition after all this time, and silly to have
been so wildly optimistic. Granted, she'd come prepared

with a small tent in case the house *had* been left to the
elements or used for animals, but all the time she'd rather
discarded the possibility in her mind and imagined it
would be simple, yet habitable.

Her father had repeated Maria's tales of the Vronda
valley and its beauties, and of her little cottage. There
were fields, olive and orange groves belonging to it.
Maria's father had been a shepherd who ran his flock on
the higher mountain pastures in the summer months, and
there were various tracks which had become his by right
of use over the years. It had sounded lovely, and her
expectations had been unfairly raised. If the house was in
such a bad state, she'd have to find lodgings in the village.

'Get in,' called Kastelli. 'I'll take you back to Agios
Nikolaos.'

'No, thank you,' she said as pleasantly as she could.
'I'll stay in Vronda.'

He came nearer. 'There's no route to it from here,' he
snapped.

'Yes, there is,' she declared, showing him the map.

He gave a small, derisive laugh. 'That's out of date.
The road is now overgrown, and much of it has subsided.
You can't go up that way. There's a new tarmac road
from the next valley, approaching Vronda through the
pass.'

She looked at the site and examined the contours carefully. The village seemed to be set on terraces down a hillside.

'I could walk up that,' she said scornfully.

'But you won't,' he said with menace. 'You would be
trespassing on my land, and I will not allow that. Besides,
the village is half-deserted. There are few people there,
and they won't take you in. Strangers are not welcome.'

'You can say that again,' she snapped.

'With good reason! We had some tourists setting light

to the trees last year. We almost lost part of a primeval forest,' he said grimly.

'That's hardly likely to happen in this rain, is it?' she said coolly.

He bit back an exclamation, his nose and mouth curved into a sneer.

'You don't seem to realise,' he seethed. 'I am late for a dinner appointment and yet I am offering to drive you some distance to the town so that you can be in comfort.'

'How generous. But I want to be here,' she said quietly. 'I have a tent, and I'm used to roughing it.'

The two men exchanged glances, and it seemed that Kastelli's brain was working overtime, thinking up more excuses. But she was wrong; he shrugged his shoulders and spread his hands in defeat.

'All right,' he said laconically. 'As you wish. I'll take you to Maria Zakro's house. But when you have seen it, I can confidently predict that you will wish you'd never bothered.'

CHAPTER THREE

HELEN lowered her eyes and considered his offer thoughtfully, pushing a loose stone around with the toe of her boot.

'Dammit, woman! I'm in a hurry! Make up your mind!' he growled.

She cocked her head on one side and insolently assessed his intentions. They didn't *seem* to include a sexual threat. He wasn't leering at her as if he wanted to get her in the back of the truck and have his evil way. Mind you, that wasn't surprising, since she looked like a drowned rat—and it was irritating that the rain merely made *him* look even more moody and magnificent!

'OK,' she said casually, as if she were doing him a big favour. 'If it'll make you happy.'

With a suppressed snarl, Kastelli reached out a hand for her rucksack and she shrugged the pack off with surprise, not expecting to be helped with it. On the evidence so far, his manners left a great deal to be desired. He muttered a few words to the guard, who tugged at the peak of his cap with a deferential gesture and held open the door for Helen.

Dimitri's powerful, intensely masculine body slid on to the seat beside her and he unzipped his leather jacket, throwing it into the back with her rucksack. Helen's eyes widened at the tight play of muscles under the snowy white shirt, and the tanned, corded arms as he rolled up his sleeves to the elbows. She knew he wasn't interested in her, and yet she could sense his potent lure. What would

34

he be like when he wanted to attract a woman?

His oak-coloured arms were glossy with black hairs like
the ones emerging from the deep open neckline. As he
started the car, she wondered idly about his sex-life. She
couldn't imagine any woman daring to think herself good
enough for him. He was so arrogant and . . . superior.
And aloof. A man who was somehow untouched by
others.

She cast a surreptitious glance at his stony profile. 'Do
you live up here?' she asked politely. It was the bounden
duty of hitch-hikers to chat to drivers.

'Sometimes.'

The tone wasn't encouraging. For a while she peered,
like him, at the road, wondering how on earth he could
drive at such a pace. She supposed he must know every
pot-hole intimately.

'In Vronda, or somewhere up the gorge?' she
ventured.

'You're not to go into the gorge,' he warned. 'It's
extremely dangerous at this time of year with rock-falls
and so on. Limestone is a notoriously unstable rock.'

'Fancy!' She knew all about rock; it was her business
to. 'What's your name?'

'Why do you want to know? What does it matter?'

She gaped at his appalling lack of courtesy. 'And I
thought Cretans were renowned for their friendliness and
generosity,' she said pointedly to herself.

Pride made him wince, and a high colour tinged his
cheekbones. 'I am Dimitri Kastelli,' he answered,
watching her closely.

'I'm Helen Summers,' she offered, and noticed that the
tense hands on the steering wheel relaxed. She contemplated a few topics of conversation and decided on the
banal. Anything else might be controversial and make
him snap at her again, and she wasn't in the mood for

bad-tempered men. 'Awful weather.'

'A freak spring. It's going to rain for weeks, I understand.'

'Oh, no!' she groaned. That settled it, she couldn't stay in the little tent in the rain for that long, she'd go mad. It was all thoroughly depressing.

'There it is,' he said, sounding satisfied. 'Down on the right.'

Helen let out a gasp of dismay. 'But it's . . . it's just a one-roomed hut!'

'I told you. Want to drive up to it, or shall I turn around now and take you back to town. I can get you there in twenty minutes to half an hour.'

She bit her lip, staring at the dilapidated hovel, whose rough, tumbled stone walls were in a bad state of repair. Only half of the roof remained, and rain beat into the upper room. Tears started in her eyes. To think that her mother had lived here! No wonder she had been tempted by the bright lights of the little tourist resort, and her father's relative wealth. Poor Maria. It must have been a difficult life. And yet, by moving away, she'd only made things worse. It must have been shattering to discover that she was pregnant, and it had been a very brave decision to make the journey to England. What a calamity, then, to go all that way, only to be desperately homesick! A wave of sympathy for her misguided mother was followed by a feeling of self-pity drawing a shuddering sob from her lips.

The truck rolled to a halt and there was a silence while Helen tried valiantly to stop the tears from tumbling down her cheeks.

'Don't do that,' growled Dimitri.

'I'm trying not to!' she muttered crossly, crying harder.

Gentle hands undid her anorak hood and drew it down.

Her thick golden plait snaked out over her shoulders, and she felt Dimitri's eyes lingering on her. He placed awkward hands on her shoulders.

'Don't cry,' he said in his low-pitched voice. 'You won't miss anything by not staying in this valley. I know somewhere you can go in town. A friend of mine owes me a favour and won't charge you. It'll be more fun there, anyway. Nothing happens here.'

The warmth of his hands began to penetrate the thin waterproof and it felt pleasant. 'I'm sorry,' she sobbed. 'I'm usually very cheerful and optimistic. I've had a few shocks lately. Things haven't been easy. Such a lot has happened . . .' He was waiting for her to gather herself together. She fumbled in her pockets for a handkerchief in vain and was handed a big white one. 'This isn't *like* me!'

'Better?' he murmured, taking the handkerchief from her fumbling fingers and wiping her eyes carefully.

Helen's wide eyes watched him. He was frowning slightly in concentration as he gently slicked away the tears, running the handkerchief down the sides of her nose and over the cleft above her top lip. His fingers slowed as her full lips parted, and she found that she was mesmerised by the incredibly sexy lift of his lashes that left them both staring deeply into each other's eyes.

'Much, thank you,' she breathed, astonished by the almost shocking impact of his nearness. Quickly she looked out of the window, trying to pull herself together. She was supposed to *like* her mother's people, not find the men incredibly attractive! It was humiliating to find herself secretly responding to the local bully, even if he was ashamed now that he'd upset her, and had decided to make amends.

'Good. I'll see if I can turn around.'

'Just a minute, please,' she said wearily. She wanted time to think and he wasn't giving her any.

His impatient check on the time was transparently for her benefit. 'I haven't long,' he frowned.

'You're rushing me. I . . .' As she'd been speaking, Helen's eyes had wandered across the valley. The village was missing! It should be opposite! She stiffened and sat up smartly.

'Something wrong?' he murmured in concern.

'You bastard!' she breathed. Something *was* wrong, very wrong!

'I beg your pardon?' he said icily, losing his air of sympathy.

Helen hastily pulled her map out of her pocket and examined it, noticing out of the corner of her eyes that Dimitri's thigh muscles were tensing. And well they might!

'I'm sorry your hearing is poor. I called you a bastard,' she said through her teeth. 'Mr Kastelli, I don't know what you're trying to do, or why, but that is not Maria's house.'

She thought she detected a flash of alarm in his eyes before the thick fringe of lashes flickered downwards to hide them.

'Of course it is.'

'No. If it were, we'd be able to see the village. Look, they're directly across the valley from each other.'

'Where *did* you get that map?' he glared.

'Where do you think?' she countered.

'It's very old.'

'The house and village aren't likely to get up and walk, even after a number of years,' she said sarcastically.

'What makes you think that particular building you keep pointing to on your map is Maria's?'

'I have it on the best authority,' she said sweetly.

'Maria,' he whispered, his lips whitening.

Heavens! thought Helen. What on earth is happening?

Mentioning her mother's name certainly brought on some odd reactions! There must be some skeleton in the Zakro family cupboard that her father didn't know about. That was awful. It would make it more difficult for her to integrate successfully.

She could almost see the wheels whirring in Dimitri's brain as he stared blankly through the windscreen.

'Yes. I could be wrong,' he said slowly. 'I think I have muddled the two buildings in my mind. Sorry. Her house must be the one further up the valley, as you say.'

'Then how about taking me there?' she said coldly. He was wriggling out of admitting that he'd lied. Too proud to acknowledge his mistakes, she supposed. What a despicable man he was!

Biting his lower lip, Dimitri released the handbrake with evident reluctance. Helen could almost see his brain working; despite his implacable façade, there was patently an awful lot of activity going on inside his skull! When they finally drove off at a snail's pace—presumably to give him more time to hatch some other devious scheme—Helen leaned back against the seat, exhausted. Talk about difficult! This man was being as obstinate and cussed as he possibly could. She was certain that he had deliberately tried to trick her. Why? What was he hiding? And what was to be gained by such a move? The prospect of what she would find at her destination made her tremble.

'Cold?' he asked, turning on the heater.

'No. Very angry,' she answered curtly.

His expression was inscrutable. They drove on in an uncomfortable silence until Helen saw the hills on either side becoming steeper, and then above the thickly clustering olive trees she could see white buildings, scrambling down narrow terraces on her left. Instinctively she looked to the right of the road; they rounded a curving hill and there was her mother's house, set as she'd imagined it, in lush fields and groves.

Her whole body slumped with relief. It looked in reasonable order. In fact, when Dimitri had grimly unlocked the door with her key, she was astonished at its condition.

They were in a large room which was obviously used as a living- and dining-room. By the fast fading light of day she could see that the walls were plain lime-washed and the ceiling lined with heavy honey-coloured cypress beams, whose fragrance she could smell already. The floor was concrete, but there were small, hand-woven rugs on it, and simple though comfortable furniture. She wandered over to the door at the back of the room, expecting to see stairs, but then she remembered the stone steps outside which would lead to the bedroom above. This door then, opened on to a marble-floored scullery, rather primitive, but perfectly adequate.

There was no smell of damp, none of that stuffy, unlived-in feeling that she had expected. After all, it had been some weeks since her father had terminated the rental.

'It looks as if someone's been living here!' she cried, turning to Dimitri, who'd gone back to collect her bag.

He slammed the door shut with a sullen look and dropped the rucksack on the floor, staring around the room.

'It's been rented out,' he said in a non-committal tone.

'They must have left very recently. It seems well-aired.'

'We have a good climate here.'

'You've just told me it's been raining,' she said sardonically.

He shrugged. 'Perhaps the people came in to tidy up,'

he suggested.

'Do you know who? I'd like to thank them for keeping it so nice,' she asked.

'Why should I know what goes on here?'

Helen's eyes widened at his rudeness.

'Too proud to mix with the peasants?' she asked coolly. 'Never mind, I'll find out without your help. I wonder whether there'll be any bedding,' she added, almost to herself.

'In the big chest under the window.'

Dimitri had answered automatically, without thinking, as if he knew the house well, and that surprised her after his claims to the contrary.

'How do you know where the bedding is kept?' she asked. 'Have you been in here lately?'

He scowled. 'You always store things like that there. It's tradition.'

Helen wasn't convinced. She wandered around, touching things: the hand-carved chairs, the wooden fruit bowl. Could those have been made by her grandfather? she wondered. A little chill swept through her body and she shivered.

Her eyes rested on the minute iron contraption on stumpy legs in the middle of the room. A tall pipe came out of it and disappeared through the ceiling.

'Can you show me how to light the stove?' she asked politely. One of them might as well show a few manners! 'Do you know how it works?'

'No,' he said, meeting her challenging eyes.

'You liar,' she retorted calmly, eliciting a wince from him.

His grin surprised her. 'I'll check the water for you.' He disappeared into the scullery and she could hear him moving things around.

'There isn't any,' he called.

Helen hurried in to see, and frowned when only a small dribble came out of the taps. 'Where's the stopcock?' she asked suspiciously.

'Stop what? Is it something to do with the plumbing?' he asked, a gleam in his eyes.

'It's . . .' She realised he was being difficult and gave up. He wouldn't tell her, even if he did know. 'So you won't help me to get warm, and I'm left without water. What do you suggest I do? Stand in the rain and open my mouth?' she snapped with uncharacteristic sarcasm.

He shrugged gracefully, trying to hide a smirk. 'There's a spring at the end of the field behind the house.'

Her eyes narrowed. 'I thought you didn't know this place.'

'I know all the springs. Everyone does,' he said with a bland expression.

'Well, bully for you,' she muttered crossly.

What else might she be deprived of? Light? Electricity? Her hand snaked out to flick on the light switch. That didn't work either, so she searched fruitlessly for candles.

'Damn!' she breathed, pausing to think.

'Bit primitive for you?' he enquired softly, lounging negligently against the door. Helen tried not to let the tingle travel too far through her body when she looked up at him. One of his dark brows was arched and he looked corrupt, wicked and very interesting. What on earth was the matter with her? She liked *nice* people, not cold-hearted lying renegades. This man looked as if he led the local wolf pack.

'Aren't you in a hurry? Your supper must be ready. Haven't you got someone cooking in a pot for you at home?' she countered.

He chuckled in delight, and Helen was treated to a display of perfect, white teeth. All capped, of course, she told herself. It was no effort, acquiring good teeth if you were rich. All you did was sign the dentist's bill. She tried to picture him without his teeth and failed, discovering instead that her eyes had locked on to his suddenly sensual mouth and his perfect teeth were glistening at her.

'They're all mine,' he murmured, roaring with laughter at her guilty, tell-tale blush. His amused eyes softened and grew more compelling under her fascinated gaze.

Helen felt a quiver of warmth drive through her and resented his potency. He had no business to be standing there exuding sex appeal when she was fed up and angry!

'They're very tempting,' she said levelly, pleased that he was momentarily disconcerted. Then he recovered and masked his real feelings again.

'Tempting?' he drawled.

'Yes,' she answered, savagely delighted at the opportunity to put him down. 'I'm tempted to give myself the great satisfaction of punching you in the mouth and smashing your smug look with one blow.'

He was vastly amused in an infuriatingly patronising way. 'Such violence! What a little temper we have,' he mocked. 'Just because things don't go your own way.'

'Why don't you go yours and leave me in peace?' she grated. 'You're supposed to be late for something, I believe.'

'I am, very, though this has been much more entertaining,' he smiled, his dark eyes laughing at her. 'Contrary to hints of cannibalism, I have a delicious fish soup, pork *souvlaki* with herbs and artichokes waiting for me. With perhaps a little flaky pastry stuffed with almonds and apricots to follow. How about you? Got a cordon bleu meal to prepare, have you?' he asked innocently.

Her mouth drooled at his description. She thought of the boring temporary rations she had brought, all of which needed heat. She'd have to try lighting the stove; it couldn't be beyond an intelligent girl like her.

'I have something rather special lined up, yes, and I'd like to get on with it,' she said airily.

'Good. In that case, I'll leave you,' he said, walking to the door. *'Bon appetit.* And sleep well. Oh, by the way, we've been having a series of rather strong earthquakes lately. Don't be too scared if we have one in the night. They only destroy cities and so on every few hundred years.'

'Oh, yes? Like to tell me when the last severe one was?' she asked drily, knowing the likely answer.

A brief smile flitted across his darkly handsome face. 'Sixteen hundred and something. Goodnight.'

The door closed behind him and Helen let out a breath she'd been storing up. What was the penalty in this country for murder? she wondered savagely, wrenching open the stove door. All her life, wherever she went, people were always pleasant to her, and she wasn't used to rudeness. Kastelli's lack of response to her had disturbed her vanity, and his bad manners had made her feel distinctly uncomfortable and unwelcome.

Her father had said that people responded positively to her because she'd inherited his sunny nature, charm and open, honest face. Although she'd hooted with laughter and told him he looked like a blond Al Capone on a bad day, she knew he was right. Yet Kastelli was immune to her friendly personality. He was being as unpleasant as he possibly could, and that had riled her.

It was getting darker. She must light the stove soon or she wouldn't be able to see a thing. With a resigned sigh she dragged her hood up over her head, picked up a torch, and took a saucepan down the field to fill with water, her eyes straining in the dusk to see where she was going. The spring came gushing from the rock and was as cold as ice.

When she returned, she stripped off the dripping stormcoat and hung it on the plank door, fetching brushwood and old newspaper from the scullery. To her immense relief, the stove was soon giving out a warm glow and she was able to add larger branches.

Whoever had used this house had left it in good order, with a large stack of dry kindling and wood in readiness for the next tenant. Of course, she could have managed, camping in her tent, if just to spite Dimitri Kastelli, but she was now so bone weary that she blessed the thoughtful person who had enabled her to light the fire so easily. The beef stew bubbled away, sending spicy smells to her eager nostrils. She thought of Dimitri Kastelli, eating his grand meal, probably surrounded by attentive servants and his subdued family. Funny, she hadn't noticed if he was married or not. But he probably was—and carefully training his sons to be as superior in attitude towards women as their father.

Helen dumped a cushion on the floor in front of the stove and curled up, peering around the room in the flickering glow and trying to imagine her mother and grandparents in these surroundings.

But tiredness had numbed her brain. After eating, she unpacked her bedroll with slow, fumbling fingers, deciding not to make a dash out into the rain and clamber up the stone steps to the upper room. It would be warmer here, anyway. She dragged off her boots and stuffed them with newspaper, laying them not too close to the fire and hanging her socks over the back of a chair. Then, with a nervous glance at the uncurtained windows, she pulled off her T-shirt and shorts, so that all she wore were her small scarlet briefs.

There was a thud outside and then another, and her heart almost seemed to stop beating as she scrambled inside the sleeping-bag for safety. Then came another

bump, and the sound of something rolling. Helen realised
with a slightly hysterical laugh that oranges were
dropping off the tree outside the front door. Her eyes
became drowsy. Tomorrow she'd sort everything out,
especially Kastelli. She remembered the ice-cold hostility
that lay barely hidden, and shivered involuntarily. He
didn't look the sort of man who liked a slip of a girl
standing up to him!

It was the heat that woke her. She'd been moving restlessly for some time, in a half-waking dream, and had
pushed down the zip of the sleeping-bag, feeling a hot
blast of air on her naked thighs. Then she became aware
of a prickling sensation that had made the hairs on the
back of her neck stand up. The air was filled with tension,
and she knew someone was in the room. Her eyes shot
open.

Dimitri was standing mesmerised at her feet, a cardboard box in his arms, his sultry eyes taking in her
abandoned pose and virtual nakedness, travelling up and
down her body in silent, hungry appraisal.

It looked as though his mouth wanted to range
uninhibitedly over her skin, and, while she stared in
numbed shock, his tongue flickered out to moisten his
lips. Helen gulped, feeling her limbs turn to water. As he
towered above her, his wide chest tapering to a narrow
waist, she noticed that he had automatically adopted a
superior masculine stance, with his legs planted firmly
apart, their muscled contours unnervingly powerful.

'Very sexy,' he drawled, making Helen's spine tingle.

But the words had also broken his magnetic spell. With
a horrified gasp, Helen hastily pulled up the sleeping-bag
to the level of her chin, blushed furiously and launched
immediately into the attack.

'You peeping Tom! How dare you? Get out of here!'

she cried, her voice cracking. She was furious with her-self. For, in the split second she had seen his raw desire, a wave of heat had engulfed her that had nothing to do with the blazing stove. Never in her life had she felt so wanton, nor experienced the extraordinary curls of heat that burnt down to her womb. Every part of her body had become sensually aware of him and of her existence as a woman. She longed to fling back the cover and lure him, to know what it was like to feel the weight of his body, the undoubtedly experienced caresses . . . Oh, God, what was she thinking of? She closed her eyes in misery, crushing the heat in her loins. 'Get out,' she whispered huskily, diverting her self-anger to him.

'You . . . are a woman,' he said in slow wonder, his voice vibrating deeply.

Her eyes snapped open. 'Top marks!' she jeered. 'Ten out of ten!' The sensual curve had gone from his mouth, to her mixed disappointment and relief.

'I thought you were just a kid earlier,' he rasped, dumping the box.

'Well, I'm not. Don't come a step nearer! How did you get in?' she demanded, holding the top of the sleeping-bag tightly up to her throat.

'I took your key with me,' he said, beginning to unpack food.

'You——' Helen was speechless.

'I had my reasons. You'll have to get used to people walking in on you anyway, if you stay in Crete. It is said that there is no word in Greek for privacy,' he said, slanting a wicked glance at her.

'Both of us are speaking English, and well know the word 'privacy',' she bit out. 'So I'll thank you to put my key on the table. Thank you. What were your reasons?'

'I thought, since the morning was chilly, you'd like me to make the room warm for you. And I brought breakfast.'

She gazed at him in astonishment. He was wearing a
cream shirt, open at the neck, and a black jumper slung
around his shoulders. His black jeans were quite old, and
he looked a little less intimidating than the previous day.

'Thought you couldn't handle stoves?' she reminded
him.

'I am an expert at lighting *some* fires. I enjoy rekindling
embers,' he said in a low voice, staring steadily into her
eyes.

Helen's breath caught in her throat. God, the man was
hypnotising her! 'I—did you say breakfast?' she croaked.

'Yes. A welcome-to-Crete apology for my behaviour
yesterday. I had an important meeting and was very tired
and preoccupied. I hope I'm forgiven?'

She supposed the important meeting had something to
do with the helicopter she'd seen, making its way up the
valley. That could explain his curtness, if he was worried
about a business problem, she thought, giving him the
benefit of the doubt. He did look penitent, despite the
piratical, raised brow. Ever ready to forgive, Helen's
smile lit up her face.

'Only if you go outside so I can get some clothes on,'
she said.

'Pity. I rather liked the idea of sitting next to those little
red knickers,' he smiled, without any sexual threat in his
expression at all.

Helen decided to take him at his face value. He did,
after all, own a large part of land here by the sound of it,
and, although she could manage without him if she had
to, it would be better if he was on her side.

'You'll sit next to a pair of grubby shorts and a red
T-shirt and like it,' she said primly.

He laughed, the rare, transforming smile making
Helen's knees weak. His serious eyes had suddenly

glowed from within, and disconcerted her.

'Do you mind if I just wait in the scullery?' he asked. 'It is chilly outside.'

She waved him in and he shut the door. When she yelled out that he could return, he seemed very pleased with himself.

'Taps work now,' he said.

A brief suspicion crossed Helen's mind. Funny how they did or didn't work every time he'd been in there. 'That's good,' she said cautiously.

His answering beam came at the same time as a shaft of sunlight angled through the window.

'Oh!' She ran over to look out. 'It's not raining! You said it would . . .' She stopped and saw his eyes drop guiltily.

'I'm sorry,' he mumbled. 'I really was trying to put you off.' His hand—ringless, she noted—thrust through his hair, turning the neat black curls into a mad riot, a totally disarming gesture that had Helen softening despite her doubts. 'Let's get the food out and into our stomachs, and I'll explain.'

He squatted on the floor and, after a moment's hesitation, Helen plumped up the cushion and joined him. He'd brought hot, crusty bread, home-made yoghurt and honey, goat's cheese, tiny tomatoes and oranges. And the flask probably held coffee.

She found that her face was creased into a broad, greedy grin. 'It's wonderful! Thank you! Er . . . can I start?'

'Be my guest,' he laughed, handing her a knife.

'Well, explain,' she mumbled, a moment later, her mouth full of bread and thyme-scented honey, 'why you've been so unfriendly.'

'It's my father, you see,' he said earnestly, stretching out his long, booted legs. 'He's been very ill—had a

couple of heart attacks that have made him very irritable.
His first one occurred last year, after he insisted on
helping to fight the forest fire in the gorge. I'm under
strict instructions to keep strangers away and be as
deceptive as necessary. Usually it doesn't take much to
put people off. You were a little more stubborn than most.
You do understand, don't you?'

How could she resist his deep, soul-searching eyes?
thought Helen in wonder. 'Yes, I suppose so.' She busied
herself with cutting chunks of cheese to dot on the soft
bread. He crossed his legs elegantly.

'Good,' he said, putting a friendly hand on her
shoulder. 'That's settled, then. I knew you wouldn't
consider going to the gorge when you realised that it
might kill him.'

Helen's mouth dropped open momentarily. It hadn't
occurred to her that was what he was getting at—she
thought he'd been apologising. Now she seemed to have
prevented herself from going into the most fascinating
part of the valley. Well, she'd let it ride for the moment,
and when he knew she was to be trusted she'd mention
her intentions. The rarest and most interesting flowers
were to be found in the gorges of Crete, some species that
existed nowhere else in the world, and she longed to trace
some so that other enthusiasts could enjoy them, too.

'So,' he said in a pleasant conversational tone, 'where
do you come from, Helen?'

'Brighton,' she said, surprised when he nodded as if he
knew of it.

'Your family are there?'

'Mmm. Well, just Dad. My mother died three months
ago.'

'I see,' he said gently. 'That's what you meant last
night about having difficulties lately. I feel an absolute
swine for upsetting you. I'll have to work hard to make up

for that!'

She moved nervously back, worried that his friendly overtures were confusing her. At the moment, she seemed to be alarmingly unstable as far as her emotions were concerned, and it would be wise to keep this man at a distance. It must be the unusual circumstances of the last few months, and his extraordinary magnetic personality that was making her so uncomfortably aware of him.

'Do you like Brighton?' he enquired politely.

'It's all right. Our home is wonderful, of course, because it's always jammed full of people. Everyone seems to use us as a meeting-place,' she laughed. 'Liz—my mother——' She looked down at the orange in her hand, hoping that he'd think her faltering voice was caused by grief. In actual fact, it was hard to think that Liz *wasn't* her mother. And she had no intention of telling anyone here about Maria, not yet. Dimitri's hand reached out and covered hers, and that made things worse, but she let it stay. 'Liz was so welcoming, you see, and Dad is so easy-going that he gets along with everyone. We've all got so many godchildren, we hire a hall on New Year's Eve and give them all a party in one go!'

'How lucky you are,' he muttered.

Helen glanced up in surprise. He was chewing his lower lip.

'Don't you have a family apart from your father?' she asked.

His hand tightened its grip. 'My mother. What made you come to Crete?'

Helen tried to work out how to answer that one.

'Oh, you know how it is: people rave about a place, you see a few photos . . .'

'People? Someone suggested you should come? A boyfriend, maybe?' His tone was one of studied casualness. Why then, thought Helen, did she get the imp-pression that she was being interrogated by a shrewd man?

'What an extraordinary question,' she fended.

'Naturally I'm interested in why people come to our island,' he said smoothly. 'Did your boyfriend say that Vronda was a pleasant place?'

The man was such an expert in fishing, she was surprised he wasn't wearing waders! 'No,' she answered brightly. Now where would he trawl? The interchange was giving her some satisfaction, because he was trying hard to hide his impatience and not succeeding very well. It seemed that she was getting under his skin!

'He didn't recommend Vronda?' he persisted.

'No.' It was going to be difficult to get rid of him, she could see that.

'How did you hear about Maria's place?'

'Why are you asking me all these questions?' she asked calmly.

'Sorry!' he laughed falsely. 'That's our way here. It's a friendly curiosity.'

'Really?'

Helen discovered, much to her confusion, that he was still holding her hand. His fingers had begun to move idly over hers, causing her skin to rise in goose-bumps.

'Is this an annual holiday from your job?' he queried, watching her intently as she nodded. 'And . . .' his fingers had moved to her palm and she tugged her hand away with indignation at his flagrant nerve ' . . . what do you do for a living?'

'I——' Hastily, Helen pushed a segment of orange into her mouth. Despite the liberties he'd been taking with her hand, she didn't think he was ready to know she was planning on bringing a score of people to his valley every month that the season lasted! 'Excuse me. My mouth was full. I work for a travel agency.'

'Interesting. You must be very good with the general

public,' he observed.

She breathed an inner sigh of relief. He thought she was a counter clerk!

'How long will you be renting this place?'

There was something odd about his tone and the way he waited for her answer, as though his whole body was tensed.

'Two months.'

She was right. His eyes had momentarily hardened. Beneath that charming façade was the same ruthless man she had met last night. Helen felt the disappointment wash through her, and realised how much she had wanted to like him. What a fool she was! Handsome, arrogant types were never nice to know; she'd met one or two before who thought they were God's gift to women, and that all they had to do was talk seductively to get everything they wanted. Trouble was, she thought gloomily, as far as Dimitri was concerned, she'd nearly fallen for his velvet voice!

'That's a long holiday,' he observed lightly, though Helen could hear the strain behind the words.

'I was very distressed when my mother died,' she said truthfully.

'Oh, yes, of course. Poor Helen.' His dark eyes held hers, and she was floundering again in their liquid depths as he lifted her hand and kissed it gently. 'If you've had enough to eat, why don't we go outside and take a walk? I expect it will be warmer now, and I'm sure you'd like some fresh air.'

She had jumped up in pleasure, a happy smile on her face, before she knew what she was doing. Because he had turned to push the remnants of their breakfast into a cardboard box, he didn't notice how her face fell as she realised he'd twisted her around her his little finger again. Well, she'd appear to play along, but wouldn't let him get away with anything. Dimitri Kastelli might be an expert in prising out secrets and seducing women, but he'd met his match in her!

CHAPTER FOUR

WHEN she stepped out of the door, Helen was stunned by the beauty of the scenery. Everything was clear, as it often is after heavy rain, the bright green hills ablaze with yellow broom. Across the valley and its groves of olive trees rose the terraced slopes of Vronda, the tiny white houses glistening in the early morning sunshine.

She could hear the clunk of sheep bells and then a donkey braying. Despite her antagonism towards Dimitri, she couldn't resist smiling up at him and hugging herself when she recognised the continual drone of bees. Bees meant flowers! And there in front of her, under the fruit trees, the wild flowers spread so thickly that they appeared to be a continuous patterned carpet, stretching as far as the eye could see: wild pea, anemone, tassel hyacinth, the buttercup-yellow pheasant's eye . . . Paradise!

'Oh, it's heavenly!' she breathed, drinking in the clean, unpolluted air.

On the gentle breeze wafted the aroma of herbs: thyme, oregano and sage, rosemary, savory . . . Helen's tiny curvy body whirled around a full circle. The field she had struggled through in the dark turned out to be a meadow, the grass all but drowned in dense scarlet waves of corn poppies. Her eyes were alight with happiness as they surveyed the scene, and her hands clasped involuntarily in delight at the squabbles of a noisy chorus of buntings, flitting in the out of the dark carob trees close by.

Helen leaned against the rough warm wall of her house,

54

quite overwhelmed.

'How incredibly beautiful it all is! It's the sort of place I've always dreamed of! I'm going to have a wonderful time here,' she said softly, deeply happy that she could easily fall in love with her mother's home.

'I'm glad you appreciate the valley,' said Dimitri in a richly vibrant voice.

Uncertainly she turned her head to look at Dimitri, expecting to find a sardonic smile on his face, but she saw what could have been approval. Then, before she could be sure, his lids dropped over his eyes and he thrust his hands into his pockets.

'Well, shall we go?' he suggested cheerfully.

'I'd love to, but actually, I need supplies from the village, thanks all the same,' she said with great reluctance. 'I ought to stagger up that hill and buy some food and a few other things. I was stupid not to bring any candles. I can't keep going to bed at eight o'clock!'

'The village?' His brows had drawn together as if he had no intention of allowing her to go there. 'I don't . . .' He seemed to correct himself. 'I don't think I can let you trail all the way up there alone,' he said. 'Why don't you let me drive you?' He held up his hand at Helen's protest. 'No, please. My forfeit for last night. OK?'

She didn't know what to make of him. Her instinct told her he was not to be trusted, and yet she also had the impression that he liked her and was struggling with some principles of his own which made him wary. Despite his currently charming smile and pleasant invitation, she knew that he hadn't wanted her to visit the village—certainly not alone, and had therefore been forced to escort her. But his eyes were deeper mirrors of his mind, and told her that he found her attractive and interesting. It was all very odd.

Caution and curiosity battled within her—curiosity

won! After all, she was quite adept at fending off his queries, and by accepting a lift she'd save herself a lot of time and effort. And maybe she'd discover a few facts about Dimitri Kastelli!

'Thanks,' she said. 'Wait a second while I find a couple of carrier bags.'

As they drove off, she remembered that the previous evening he'd claimed the village road entered from the other side of the hill. It seemed that hadn't been a lie, after all, because they were apparently driving all the way out of the valley and into the next one. It seemed a terribly roundabout way to reach a village which was only up the hill!

'Why isn't the old, more direct route to the village used any more?' she asked, voicing her thoughts.

'It was always unstable. Because of the differing layers of rock, there are places on the hillside where water collects and gushes out as springs. It became a major job every year to repair the road, and it was often washed away—sometimes immediately after it had been rebuilt. When my father bought the hillside below Vronda, the villagers agreed that he could build them another road. They don't mind. Those with motorised transport can use it, those without still walk the donkey trail.'

'And you?' she asked, wondering where he lived, but not daring to ask. Despite opening up a little just now, he looked very forbidding. He was tense, as if alert for trouble, and she didn't want to cross him!

'I drive, sometimes I walk,' he said curtly.

Helen's face softened. He couldn't be too bad then, if he enjoyed walking in this glorious valley! She was sure that a man like him would only choose to walk for pleasure and not necessity.

'I don't think I've ever known such a lovely valley,' she said dreamily. 'I've walked through the Lake District and Wales, Scotland, Dorset . . . oh!' Helen almost told him about the foreign countries she'd worked in, but something held her back. 'Well, this is my favourite.'

'Vronda is honoured.'

He gave a slow, rare grin that somehow reached into her very core and left her shaky. Helen had never known a man with such hidden depths. The little glimpses she'd had of his private self were fascinating, and she wanted to wipe away his surface reserve and plumb those depths. He would be an interesting man to know, she mused.

She enjoyed the trip enormously. Refreshed by the rain, the silver-leaved olive trees rustled in the breeze. Overhead, sickle-winged swifts soared and dived in the heavily scented air. By the time Dimitri turned off the main road she had spotted so many varieties of wild flowers that her head reeled with their names. He had laughed as she'd hung out of the window, peering at isolated specimens.

'What are you doing?' he chuckled. 'Isn't your face cold?'

'Freezing,' she admitted, reluctantly winding up the window against the chill wind blowing from the north. She hadn't realised how much Vronda was protected. 'But I'm flower-spotting.'

'Plenty of those everywhere,' he said. 'The valleys are renowned for them.'

'Oh? And the gorge?' she asked casually.

'Too cold and dark,' he said quickly. 'Unattractive place.'

'You live up there, don't you?'

'Yes. This is the Vronda road. A good one, isn't it?'

Helen assented, vowing to get up that gorge if it was the last thing she did! She didn't believe him for one moment about it being dangerous. Of course, she had to be careful that his father didn't get upset, but he was being ridicu-

lously protective. No one was going to have a heart attack
at the sight of a five-foot blonde!

They crested the hill at the top of the village, and
Dimitri parked the truck.

'Pedestrians and donkeys only in Vronda,' he said, in
answer to her raised eyebrows. 'The streets are steps.'

Helen looked more closely and saw that they were. But
even more surprising was the fact that they were
overgrown with crown daisies and wild gladioli, and the
whole place looked very unkempt. As they walked
downhill, she saw that the houses on either side were
deserted, their only inhabitants the little linnets who were
singing so joyously. A chill ran through her. What were
his intentions? Perhaps she had been foolish to trust him.

'Wait a minute,' she said, stopping dead in her tracks.
'No one lives here.'

'No. Many of the villagers have gone away. But there
are still some families living around the church, and that's
where we're heading. Do you think I'm lying?' he asked,
seeing her disbelieving look.

'It wouldn't be the first time,' she reminded him.

He gave a disarming smile. 'I explained all that,' he
said easily. 'I thought I was forgiven. Shall I pop home for
my sackcloth and ashes?'

'I doubt such things are in your wardrobe,' she said
drily, and was pleased to see that he could take a joke
against himself.

'Don't you remember my supper?' he murmured. 'A
disobedient slave, simmering in the pot? There'll be a few
ashes underneath, I'm sure.'

Helen gurgled with laughter. 'You are the most extraordinary man,' she observed, beginning to walk down the
hill again.

'And you, Helen Summers, are the most . . .' His avid
eyes devoured her like a theatrical lecher, his eyebrows

waggling alarmingly and sending Helen into peals of laughter.

'You are silly,' she giggled.

'Hmmm. I can honestly say that you are the first person ever to call me silly.'

'I bet. You've got an extremely intimidating, glacial look about you sometimes,' she grinned, following his long, lithe stride. 'What's that noise?'

She could hear a strange creaking sound—or were they coughs? Dimitri led her to the village cistern, and she peered in to see huge bullfrogs complaining to each other.

He was standing on the edge of a terrace. 'Look at the view,' he said softly.

They sat on a low stone wall, tufts of campanula sprouting from its cracks, the little lavender bells nodding in the gentle breeze. Helen looked out over the empty silence, broken only by distant tinkling as goats grazed the lush vegetation. Ahead were the jagged peaks of the Thripti mountains, topped by an icing of snow. Dark birds with huge wingspans hovered high over the peaks—far too high for her to identify them.

To her ears came the plaintive sound of *bouzouki* music, oriental, rich in sensuality and lending an unreal quality to Helen's surroundings. And, like an improbable jewel perched on the flank of the hill, there stood a tiny, dazzlingly white Byzantine church with coral-tiled roof and a small round tower.

'Can we go in?' she asked eagerly, indicating it.

'If you like. I have the key,' he said, uncurling his long legs.

They wandered down a narrow path through an exuberant display of tea-plate-sized mauve daisies.

'Hottentot figs!' cried Helen in delight, after racking her brains for a moment.

'What?' Dimitri's puzzled face made her laugh.

'The flowers,' she explained.

'You know quite a lot about flowers, don't you?' he said quietly.

'A fair bit,' she said, urging him to unlock the door of the little church. It seemed very parochial to her, having your own key, and only served to remind her of his importance in this valley.

'Stay here or you'll stumble over something. Wait while I light the oil lamp.'

He left her in the doorway, but already her eyes were becoming accustomed to the dark and were discovering that the whole of the tiny church, its ceilings, pillars and walls, were covered in the most wonderful frescos.

'Dimitri!' she gasped. 'You never said . . . They're lovely, they . . . Oh, what a marvellous surprise!'

How nice he looks, she thought with a sudden shock, as he stood in front of the altar, smiling at her delight. Gone was the aloof restraint and the air of harsh self-discipline. He was almost glowing with pleasure. Helen's heart surprised her with a sudden flip.

'We're very proud of the frescos,' he said warmly.

'Tell me about them.' She began to wander around, examining each scene with great interest.

'They're all fourteenth century, painted by a man called Christofides. This one shows the inside of the church itself. It hasn't changed at all, has it?'

'The men are all standing in the front and the women at the back!' cried Helen. 'Does that happen now? Men and women separated, I mean?' she asked, round-eyed.

'Of course. Have to keep the women in their place,' he said, straight-faced, and grinning when she gave him a playful glare. 'How could a man keep his thoughts on God, Helen, if he has a pocket Venus beside him?' he murmured with a meaningful lift to his eyebrow.

Her look was scathing. But she felt ridiculously pleased that he thought of her in that way.

'Strangers, though,' he continued, 'are given a place in the front, a place of honour. They come from God, you see.'

'That's lovely,' said Helen. 'And I must say, I like the way someone has put flowers by all the icons. Wild lilies, iris, poppies, and look at all these huge daisies!'

She fell into a reverie, placing her mother in one of the pews and visualising her grandparents there, too. It gave her a good feeling. When they came out into the sunlight and walked around the other side of the church, she saw they were in a small square, edged with naked, coppiced mulberry trees, their whitewashed trunks rising from rich red earth. Little houses with plain wooden doors enclosed the square, one of them with an open door showing a tiny courtyard beyond laden with a profusion of plants.

'That's the taverna,' said Dimitri. 'Shall we have a drink?'

'Lovely,' smiled Helen. But it wasn't.

At first, in her happy mood, she didn't notice anything unusual. They sat under a small canopy of reeds, with tiny slivers of light shafting through. Still enchanted with everything around her, she chattered eagerly to Dimitri after the silent owner had taken their order for Greek coffee.

A glass of water was placed by each cup and plates of *mezes*, the snacks which she'd heard accompanied every drink. With enthusiasm she tucked into the sunflower seeds and nuts, and dunked the long green beans into a herby dressing. Gradually she became aware that there were few people around, only catching the occasional glimpse of a long black skirt around a corner or a stocky figure disappearing into one of the houses further up the next terrace.

'This is a very rich valley,' she said. 'Why did the people move away? What happened?'

'My father,' he said. 'He bought up the valley field by field, and the villagers who sold up to him had insufficient land to grow their crops or feed their stock.'

'That's terrible!' she frowned.

'Not really,' he said wryly. 'They charged him the most outrageous prices, and settled to live like kings elsewhere.'

'What do the people do who are still here?'

'Work for my father, mostly. Either on the land, in the house or at sea. Beyond the hills lies the Aegean. Our land runs to the shore.'

'You must be very wealthy.' Helen had never met anyone who owned so much land. 'What does your father do, to be so rich?'

Shutters came down over his face. 'Nothing. He once owned the village taverna here. He married money,' replied Dimitri laconically.

'Oh, how awful!' she blurted out, and then flushed with embarrassment. 'I'm sorry——'

'Don't be,' he said abruptly. 'You could be right.'

Helen never forgot how uncomfortable and awkward she began to feel, sitting in the sunshine, looking out over the valley to the high mountains and down on her little white house. It happened gradually and subtly, but soon she felt that hostility was being directed at them both from the villagers. One or two passed, silently fingering their worry beads: wary, suspicious and with a consciously proud tilt to their heads. Naturally she gave them a broad smile and a greeting; they looked her up and down with their dark, slow gazes, and gave the briefest of nods, ignoring Dimitri altogether.

'Why don't they like me?' she whispered to Dimitri, after a Cretan woman had sullenly replenished their cups of strong, sweet Greek coffee and acted as if they weren't even sitting there.

Dimitri's brooding black eyes scanned the lurking people with apparent indifference, a glint appearing within them as they suddenly stopped staring at him and became very busy.

'Perhaps I shouldn't have brought you. You might have

been better on your own. But they might have worried to see a stranger up here. Few penetrate the valley.'

'I'm not surprised,' said Helen wryly.

'Well, don't take their reticence personally. It's me they don't like. They resent the Kastellis.'

He sounded so bitter and sad that she reached out and grasped his hand before she knew what she'd done. It was in her nature to be warm and generous, and she hated people to be unhappy. For all his wealth and superb good looks, he'd missed out on one or two of the best bits in life. His eyes met hers and sparks flashed from them. Helen's hand trembled, but he had taken it in his and was holding it gently.

'Are you usually this forward?' he murmured.

'Don't get the wrong idea,' she said quickly, her heart hammering to feel his touch. She'd wanted that contact, wanted more, in fact. It was a need she'd never experienced with such uncontrollable fervour. 'I'm a toucher, like my father. If I feel friendly towards people, I like to make a physical contact.' Her throat had become parched as she spoke and, although she'd said those very words often before, they'd never seemed so sensual. 'People like being touched,' she said firmly.

'I've never liked it.' He smiled into her eyes. 'Until now.'

'You're flirting,' she reproved, trying to draw her hand away.

'I do hope so,' he chuckled.

'It's outraging everyone.' Helen disliked being stared at. 'They're looking at us as if we were strangers from another planet indulging in questionable behaviour.'

'Anything I do is questionable as far as they're concerned,' sighed Dimitri.

'Why?' Helen was fascinated. He was the local bad boy, from the sound of it!

'Well . . .' He contemplated the salt and pepper which

he'd lined up on the table with the sugar. His eyes lifted to Helen's open, trusting face, and there was a softening within them. 'My father caused a stir when he married the wealthy widow whose car broke down on the road beyond. He was strong and handsome, very virile, and made an immediate impact on her.'

If he was anything like Dimitri, thought Helen, she knew how that wealthy widow felt!

'The people here,' continued Dimitri, 'despised the way he chose to realise his vaunting ambition. The problem is that I never mixed with the villagers; we're strangers, and they'd made their minds up to hate me before I was even born. My mother sent me to board at a school in Athens. I hated it, every damn second I was there.' He gave a brief laugh. 'Now, why am I telling you all this?' he wondered.

'Perhaps because I could be one of the few people you can't bully,' she laughed, trying to lighten the tone. 'Let's get my supplies—if they'll sell me anything.'

'They wouldn't refuse,' he said quietly, his mouth determined. 'No one refuses the Kastellis. No one has ever crossed us and won. I have never been thwarted. I hope you appreciate that fact.'

She nodded, feeling the back of her neck grow cold. His tone had become slightly menacing, and she was sure that he was warning her. If she was to get what *she* wanted, she'd have to go very carefully indeed.

Later, when he had left her at the house, she wondered at his attitude. Now she thought about it, he'd been definitely on the defensive when he'd walked into Vronda square, as if expecting antagonism. And he hadn't tried to be friendly at all to the people. He'd spoken curtly, without any expression on his face whatsoever. What an odd man he was—cold and silent, and yet with passions running deep, she was sure. And what a bleak picture he had painted of his childhood! She wouldn't exchange her simple life for his!

CHAPTER FIVE

DURING the next few days, Helen enjoyed herself immensely, photographing the flowers in the meadows and hills close to the house. There were plenty of unusual ones to keep her happy, and she found some rare orchids on the overgrown track that had once led up to Vronda.

Each morning when she woke, she took her simple breakfast of bread, honey, yoghurt and fruit out to the low stone wall, and sat there listening to the soaring larksong backed by the continual, vibrating hum of countless bees. It was a wonderful way to begin the day. It was as if time stood still. The pace of life was so slow that it seemed almost as if she were living in a dream, and Helen soon felt that she was held fast by the magic of Vronda. It would be hard, having to leave. But, she grinned in delight, the house would always be waiting for her! Her father could come on holiday here—they could arrange transport for him, and she could find some way of getting him around. The future opened out in a wonderful pattern; they had been happy before, but owning this house and land made Helen feel ecstatic!

After thoroughly investigating the donkey paths which meandered into the hills, and noting them in her book for possible longer walks, she struck out one morning towards the sinister mouth of the gorge.

Sun ignited the brilliant yellow of the crown daisies in the orange grove, and Helen's head swam with the scent of orange blossom. Her face softened in contentment as she watched one of the villagers leading a flock of goats through the lush meadows. Early every morning, women rode out on donkeys to the fields, sitting side-saddle and leading a cow or a muzzled, fat-tailed ewe, with a small flock of goats jostling each other at the rear. In the evening, at sunset, they returned; the goats' distended udders supported by a truss so that they could walk after the day's rich grazing.

The man answered her cheery greeting with a slow, hesitant smile, and Helen was pleased. Hopefully the people here would realise she was harmless!

It took her over two hours to walk to the end of the valley, because she kept stopping to take photographs and make notes. Her book quickly filled with sketches of purple bugloss, stately asphodel, tulips, lupins and shy cyclamen, all growing wild, all delighting her eyes with their careless abundance. Her ears rang with the constant birdsong, and a backing group of droning bees.

Once she thought she saw a flash of light on the hills ahead, but, although she trained her binoculars up there, she saw nothing, and then as she lowered them she was diverted by the sight of a huge bird hovering motionless in the deep blue sky. It was a griffon vulture. Helen watched for ages and felt sorry when it effortlessly flapped its fingered wings and glided away. She was bending down and looking at an orchid through her microscope when she heard Dimitri's voice.

'Seen something interesting?'

His tone made her wary. It held a note of ice.

'Ophrys Fuciflora Forma Maxima.' She giggled at his face. 'To you, a Late Spider Orchid,' she said innocently.

His eyes were everywhere, taking in her notebook, binoculars and John Fraser's powerful camera with its special lenses.

'I'm impressed,' he said tightly, forcing a smile 'What exactly are you doing?'

'I'm making notes about the flowers.' He was beginning to spoil her lovely day with his disapproving attitude. She chewed on her lip and looked up at him from under her lashes.

'I thought you were a clerk.'

'Clerks are allowed to have hobbies.'

They were beginning to spar again, and Helen felt depressed at the prospect. She didn't want to fight him.

'And carry expensive equipment?'

'Why not?'

'You've bought all that?' His tone held a note of derision. 'A trifle extravagant.'

'Some of it belongs to a friend,' retorted Helen crossly.

'Friend? He picked up her notebook.

'Give that back!' cried Helen, outraged.

'Secrets?' he mocked, flicking over the pages.

'It's mine! Keep your hands off my things!'

'Well, well, well!'

He'd found the page where she'd attempted to draw views. It was given a thorough inspection, and then he turned over to find small maps she'd drawn of the trails, prior to making a more detailed plan of the routes. When he looked up, her bones chilled at the hostile expression on his face.

'What are these for?' he asked in soft, sinister tones.

'N-n-none of your business!' she stuttered.

Dimitri suddenly grabbed both of her arms, and she felt his fingers bite hard into the flesh when she tried to wriggle free.

'What are you doing here?' he breathed. 'You're no ordinary tourist. Tell me what's going on!'

Her eyes crinkled up with pain, but she refused to let him know how much he was hurting her.

'What I do is none of your business! I'm a free woman and intend to stay that way. I have no wish to share confidences with you! If I want to draw this valley and write about it, that's nothing to do with you!'

'Oh, but it is,' he grated. 'Very much so. It is an invasion of privacy.'

'*Drawing?*' she scorned, with great emphasis.

'What do you intend doing with this notebook?' he snapped, shaking her slightly.

'Never mind what I intend to do with that, you ought to be worrying about what I'm going to do when you let me go,' she said grimly. 'Why don't you leave me alone? Go back to your ice palace, wherever it is up that dark and cold gorge, and let the rest of the world enjoy itself!'

The harsh, indrawn breath alerted her to the effect of her words. There was a whitening of the skin around his nostrils, and his mouth had set in a thin, hard, merciless line. His fingers tightened in fury and, despite her vow not to let him know he was hurting her, she moaned. Suddenly he realised what he was doing and seemed ashamed, thrusting her away in disgust.

'Damn you!' he muttered, glaring at her with savage eyes. 'I think you'd better answer my questions before I lose my temper.'

'Why the hell should I?' she defied, tossing her head so that the blonde plait swung violently.

'It wouldn't be wise to deny me,' he growled.

'I don't see what you could do, if I did,' she said, trembling a little when his eyes and sensual mouth spoke of demanding more than information!

'You forget, what I say goes around here. I don't often wield my authority, but it's there, nevertheless,' he said harshly. 'If I tell the villagers to refuse you supplies, you'd find it impossible to survive for long.'

'You bastard!' she spat, infuriated

'To prevent you throwing that word at me again, let me assure you I'm not. My parents were as much married as yours!' he retaliated, her wince going unnoticed. 'Well? How long do you think you can survive on your current rations?'

'Blackmailer,' she muttered, an uncharacteristically malicious streak making her decide to infuriate him with the truth. 'All right, I'll tell you, though you'll wish you'd never asked! I research and plan guided walks for the travel agency I work for. I've organised two very successful Flower Walks for botanists and flower enthusiasts in France and Madeira.' She could sense in Dimitri's silence a dangerous stillness, as if he was waiting for her to finish before he erupted, but his face was a cold mask, betraying nothing. 'Well, we're keen to investigate Crete, and this area in particular.'

'Did you say walks? You mean, strangers coming here? Holiday-makers?'

His face was a picture. Helen swallowed a grin and nodded. 'Botanists are very careful people. They care for the environment and . . .'

'*No!*' he roared, planting his legs apart and folding his arms. 'You can't do that. This land is private and I told you how excited my father would become if a little thing like you trotted around, let alone coachloads of gawping tourists!'

'Don't call me a little thing! And don't exaggerate!' she said tartly. 'There'll be small parties of hikers who'll tiptoe about without disturbing anyone. I know exactly what I can and can't do, I've studied m . . . Maria's documents. The Greek Tourist Bureau translated them for me. They confirmed that if the holder of the right of way gives permission, there's no restriction on the number of people who can travel it. There are quite a few tracks that were used by the Zakros, ones that go through your precious gorge and up to the summer pastures and I intend to walk them, photograph the flowers and views for the booklet that accompanies the walks, and eventually bring people here.'

'The area is too dangerous,' he said quickly. 'Very unsuitable for people to roam. Both Maria's parents lost their lives in a landslide up there. You can't mean to take . . .'

'I always double check for safety,' she said coldly. 'I have considerable experience in mountain and fell walking in Britain and other countries.'

'You know nothing of these hills. Take the word of someone who has lived here and knows practically every inch. This is no place for the public.'

'If that is so, then I will investigate elsewhere,' she said. 'But since I'm here, I'll make my own decisions. I never take anyone's word for anything. If the place is dangerous, then I'll see for myself.'

'You're determined to go up there?' he said grimly, waving his hand towards the dark slash in the rock.

'Of course.' Her brown eyes held his challenge. 'That will be the most interesting place, botanically speaking.'

'And Maria has given her permission?' he asked quietly.

She evaded that. 'John Fraser never proceeds without knowing that landowners and local people are perfectly happy about our walkers. We make frequent checks with the owners to make sure there aren't any problems arising.'

'I see. Close contact.'

Was it her imagination, or had a gleam of excitement run across his face? Now she couldn't see, because he had turned his back to her.

'It seems a very honourable company,' he said slowly.

'Oh, it is!' she cried, delighted that she was winning him over, her face wreathed in smiles. After all, he'd said he knew every inch . . . If he could help her, show her the best places to go, that would be wonderful! Helen smiled at her own self-deceit, knowing full well that her overriding wish was to know Dimitri Kastelli a little better and penetrate the barrier to reach the man beneath. 'Dimitri,' she coaxed, catching hold of his arm, intent on persuasion, 'you've no idea what pleasure it would give people to be able to come here! Even in the few days I've wandered around, I've been astounded at the plants I've not seen before. The place is groaning with flowers!'

'Hmm. I'm not sure.'

Yet Helen could see that he'd changed his mind and was only trying not to capitulate too easily! Playing his game, she hung on to his arm and gave an appealing smile.

'Please think about it,' she suggested. 'It'll be no bother to you, and think of the happiness you'd be spreading!'

His amused eyes looked down on her. 'I? Spread happiness?' He laughed at the idea. 'First I'll talk to my father and prepare him, in case he sees you wandering up Vronda gorge——No, wait,' he said, as her eyes lit up. 'I'm only agreeing to your *presence* there at the moment. Don't forget, if you wish to step one foot off the track before you reach the high pastures, you'll be trespassing.'

'Yes, Dimitri,' she said meekly.

'It worries me when you're submissive,' he muttered suspiciously.

'Oh, don't worry,' she grinned. 'I'm not really.'

He gave a short laugh and shook his head. 'You're impossible! How cleverly you twist me round your little finger.'

'Er . . . yes.' Helen wasn't sure she was. Somewhere in that rich, deep voice, insincerity lurked.

'So, I think perhaps you could come to a compromise, since I have,' he murmured. 'I want to show you the gorge. I'd enjoy it, and of course I couldn't let you risk any danger, and I know which trails are unsafe.'

Helen hid her pleasure and bit down the simmering excitement that had welled up inside her. This was exactly what she had hoped for!

'Fine. You can carry all my heavy stuff,' she said cheekily.

'I might bring a donkey instead,' he said drily, eyeing her bulky camera bag. 'There is one thing, you can do me a big favour. Well, it would be doing Maria a favour, in fact.'

'Oh?' She was suddenly wary. When he'd got over the shock of imagining earnest botanists in shorts tramping through his precious gorge, she really ought to tell him that Maria was dead. The constant deception was telling on her nerves.

'You could put me in touch with her. There are one or two problems about her water supply that we need to clear up. She'll have to make some decisions about installing a new system if she wants to keep renting the place out. If I get an answer from her soon then I might even be able to get my plumber to include it in the work he's doing at my house, and she'd have the work done free.'

His offer had put Helen in a very difficult situation. If it was genuine, she could save herself a lot of money. On the other hand, he could be lying about the need for a new water supply and she would have blurted out her secret before she was ready. After all, if everyone here condemned Maria, then as her daughter she would be tarred with the same brush. She decided to stall for time.

'That's difficult, I——'

'Helen,' he said, reaching out to hold her tiny waist, 'don't you want your Flower Walks to suceed? I do you a good turn, you do me one. That's fair, isn't it? Has Maria asked you to keep her whereabouts secret? You can tell me. I have learned to be very discreet. I promise you in the sight of God that I won't divulge her address to anyone.' A slight frown drew his dark brows together. 'You do know where she is, don't you?'

His eyes, his seductive voice and his warm, spreading fingers were making her tremble. Of course she could tell him, she thought hysterically. She'd visited the grave with her father.

'I——' She gulped, and then ran a tongue over dry lips.

'My God, but you're beautiful,' muttered Dimitri.

Helen was rooted to the spot in surprise. Something was

preventing her from speaking. He came closer, then pulled her hard into his body, and she thudded against him so that she was breathless for a moment. And as her mouth parted in a gasp, his dropped down to cover it: warm, hard, searching, searing her lips with a fire that crept treacherously through her body, turning the blood in her veins to a heavily throbbing and turgid mass, dazing her brain and rendering her incapable of rational thought.

From the way he was reacting, Dimitri had been ignited by the same flame. His mouth had begun to gentle, but the kisses he offered were infinitely more sweet and agonising in their intensity than before. Wanton in her abandon, Helen's arm crept around his neck as she stood on tiptoe, her breasts crushed against his hard chest.

Then he lifted his head and looked at her, bemused.

'What happened?' he asked huskily.

'You mean you don't know?' she teased, secretly unnerved by his impassioned kisses.

Dimitri grinned in delight. 'No,' he said innocently. 'Just let's go through that again, and maybe I'll catch on.'

'I think,' she said shakily, pushing him gently away, 'that far too much caught on. We've only just met, after all.'

His mouth looked impossibly sexy. She blinked and tried to fight down the longing to reach out for him.

'Come out with me tonight,' he said suddenly.

'I really don't think that's a good idea . . .'

'But you want to get to know me, don't you?' he murmured silkily, touching her face.

Her body sprang into life again and she blushed scarlet, irritated by his gentle chuckle.

'And we have to discuss your walks.'

'Oh, bother you, Dimitri Kastelli!' she laughed, ruefully knowing what her real motives were for wanting to spend the evening with him.

'Are you going to need persuading?' he murmured.

'Because if so . . .' His eyes kindled as he gently stroked her ear and bent his head towards her.

'No!' she gasped, moving back quickly. 'I'll come! To discuss my walks, you understand! Where do you suggest?'

'Somewhere we can have a long, luxurious meal and dance the night away,' he smiled. 'You choose. Anywhere you like—after all, you don't have to worry that I can afford it,' he added wryly.

'Anywhere?' she repeated. He nodded emphatically. 'Well . . . if you really mean that . . . Please, then, I've read so much about it, take me to the Cretan Palace,' she begged her eyes huge with excited anticipation. Never in her life had she thought she'd ever go there! It was one of the swankiest hotels in the Mediterranean.

'But . . .'

'I knew it! You're going to double-cross me again! No wriggling out of it!' she complained. 'You promised. And if you say it's closed or the road up to it is dangerous, then I'll struggle all the way to the village and telephone to find out if you're telling the truth!'

He shrugged. 'As you wish. Though I hear the food isn't . . . all right, all right!' he said, backing away as she advanced in mock anger. 'You'll look a bit out of place in shorts, however. Everyone else will be in diamond-encrusted gowns.

'I can't wait to see you in yours,' she murmured.

He laughed, and the momentary tension that had creased his brow eased.

'You . . . really want to go there? I do know a wonderful little . . .'

'No,' she said firmly. 'The Cretan Palace.'

It had taken Helen two hours to get ready. She felt quite idiotic, being so nervous: it was hardly her first date! But this time she knew she was going out with a man who walked alone, a man who was devious, determined and devilishly sexy. He might have made a few casual passes at her, but he still gave the impression of being in charge—and was infuriatingly controlled! Now, she thought with some sympathy, she knew how it felt to be bowled over by someone. He certainly made her insides turn to jelly.

There was far more to Dimitri Kastelli than he let on. Despite the fact that he showed interest in her as a woman, she was aware that he had never deviated from his earlier intention of finding out everything about her and Maria Zakro, and making sure that he got his own way. Whatever that was. Tonight she'd have to fight down her natural response to his sultry masculinity and manipulate *him*.

That was why she dressed to kill! He wouldn't be quite so immune by the end of the evening and she would be able to get him eating out of her hands. Normally, that was the last thing Helen wanted, but the whole of her Walks schedule depended on this. So she worked hard on her appearance.

Because her father had insisted she visited a good restaurant, she had rolled up her white Grecian dress—her one bit of glamour—tucked it in a pillow-case and pushed it into the rucksack. It was draped over a chair now, and looked as if it was fresh from the shop.

She'd spent a long time washing her hair in the spring, and discovered that the water had a miraculous effect: in the small dressing-table mirror of the bedroom she could see that her hair looked blonder, silker and sexier than ever before. Would he like it up, or loose? She experimented for ages and then gave up, letting it flow unrestrained in thick, luxuriant waves down her back.

Her skin glowed from the inner excitement that made her fingers clumsy, and when she finally drew on the dress she was almost afraid that she looked too tempting. Helen wasn't vain, but she knew she was attractive. On this occasion she wondered whether he'd take all her careful preparation as a go-ahead sign. Dimitri was the kind of man who would cynically watch a woman making 'come-hither' signals, assess her suitability in bed, take her and finally leave her without any emotion involved, or any compunction. She didn't want that. He had to want to please her, but keep a reasonable distance. She too must remember the purpose of the meal tonight, not let him divert her cleverly with sweet words and hot glances. On past performances, that was what he'd do, and she'd discover that she'd not only agreed never to darken his ravine again, but had told him who she was and sold every inch of her land! This was a business meal and she ought to remember it, she told herself sternly, tugging at the top of her dress so that less swelling flesh was around to tempt him.

It was odd how magnetic he was. She felt a little like a helpless fly mesmerised by a spider when he was around, though she was sure no fly suffered the same breathlessness that she did, nor the same elation that lit her up like a beacon. No man had made her feel like that before, with a mere look. He just stood there and she wanted to go to him. There was a glow in her heart when she thought of him, a quickening of her pulse when he . . .

'Helen! Are you ready?'

'Oh!' She jumped guiltily and ran to the window, peering down. Outside was a Porsche, the colour of chestnuts. Her knees went weak. She wasn't ready, but he was in the house downstairs and she didn't know if she ought to go out with him or not, the way she felt. In her bones she knew that something would happen tonight—she was almost wishing it to. And she had to keep cool, play the game of cat and mouse and not let him get the better of her.

It was really all impossible! She had to remember that he was being charming for a purpose, that he was up to something. Everything pointed to that. Those occasional lapses of honesty weren't necessarily typical, and you had to be careful of inveterate liars. So often she'd caught him out in a lie, or knew he was dissembling. Something more was at the bottom of his hostility to her plans, and she wanted to find out, if only to clarify their relationship.

'Helen?' Dimitri had run up the stone steps and was knocking on the bedroom door. 'Are you there?'

'Yes . . .' She was angry at the frail little voice that came out, and forced herself to do better. 'Yes, shan't be long.'

'Are you dressed?'

'Of course! I——'

The door-latch was lifted and he came in. Helen's heart hammered loudly, and her hand fluttered to her throat. Oh, hell, she thought in despair. Why does he have to look so incredibly handsome?

'Will this be all right?' she babbled, worried that he was frowning thoughtfully at her. That wasn't the reaction she'd expected! 'I ran short on the diamonds, so decided to stick with skin, bone and silk.'

He began to walk towards her, still puzzled, as if he hadn't heard. Helen backed away and he came to his senses with a jerk. 'I'm sorry, what did you say?' he asked, his eyes slowly wandering over her body.

'Skip it,' she said, disappointed that he hadn't been staggered by her beauty. The man was too immune by half! She'd never coax him to let her have her own way. Well, she could be immune, too, she lied to herself. 'You look nice.'

Nice! The dinner-suit had been poured over him, and she was sure it had been tailored to fit every individual muscle, since she was more aware of his physique than she had been before. There was something undeniably sexy about dinner-jackets anyway, and the brilliant white shirt made his face look an enviable dark gold. It wouldn't do to look at him too hard.

She searched around for things to put in her tiny white suede handbag, hoping he didn't notice that her hands kept

knocking everything over. Steady, Helen, she said to herself.
Calm down. He's only a man.

The man came close behind her, his body a hair's breadth
from her tingling back. Her breathing became erratic, and
then was cut off when she felt his fingers slipping between the
low-cut back of her dress and her blazing hot skin.

'The label was sticking out,' he said in a throaty voice.

'Oh,' she whispered.

His hands spanned her waist, and she looked into the
mirror to see his expression. It didn't reassure her. The
sultriness of his eyes had that come-to-bed look, and his
mouth was definitely sensual.

'I'm ready,' she muttered, pulling against his hands.

'So am I.' He didn't move, only held her imprisoned.
'More than ready.'

Helen set her teeth against her own liquid heat and
thought hard about his clever wiles. 'Good,' she said,
shifting her weight and pretending to stumble. Her stiletto
heel ground down into his foot and she slid away when he
reacted. 'Oh, dear,' she said, as his pained face caught her
conscience. 'I didn't mean to hurt you.'

'You're supposed to pretend that was an accident,
according to the usual rules,' he grated.

'I have my own rules,' she said grimly. 'Oughtn't we to
leave?'

'If that's what you want.'

'That's what I want,' she said, convincing herself.

It had been a narrow escape. Every second he had stayed
close to her, sending electrifying shocks through her system,
she had been on the brink of relaxing against his body and
encouraging him to explore her curves. Maybe if she had
been in the same situation with a different man she would
have allowed him a little kissing, a little touching tonight, in
order to make him her willing accomplice in her project. But
Dimitri was too dangerous to fool around with. And Helen

knew that once she aroused him, really aroused him, the animal passion that he kept under control would erupt with such an intensity that neither of them would be able to stop until they were physically sated with each other.

That would be unthinkable. It could even lead to a re-run of her mother's situation. As far as Helen was concerned, she wanted to live a life without tragedy. She wanted to marry with honour and bear children in wedlock.

Dimitri Kastelli was threatening her morality. Tonight she would have to keep a tight hold on her rocketing emotions and make sure *he* kept a tight rein on his lust.

CHAPTER SIX

HELEN followed Dimitri down the stone steps, her eyes unable to tear themselves away from the feral grace of his body. His shoulders stretched in a broad sweep immediately in front of her gaze; his narrow hips moved easily in the immaculately cut suit. Helen's fingers itched to reach out and touch the black curls which had been temporarily tamed to lie neatly against his handsome head and which finished in a smooth curve on the tanned neck. She was astonished at herself. She liked to touch people, but this was ridiculous!

Walking into the exclusive hotel with such a well-dressed yet intensely masculine man was going to be a spectacular experience! He held open the wide door of the low sports car and she crossed her fingers, hoping she'd make it to the seat with some dignity. As she swung her body around, his hand supported her elbow and he bent over her so that she could detect the subtle scent of his aftershave. It had a slightly musky aroma, and it was all she could do to prevent herself from lifting her face nearer to his to identify the brand. By the time he had settled her in, her legs were trembling from his attention and it needed all her will-power to summon up a glare when both his hands landed on either side of her seat and he dropped a kiss on her cheek.

'Not allowed?' he smiled, moving away.

'Definitely not,' she said coldly.

'Oh, dear.'

Helen deliberately looked out of the window so that she wouldn't see or sense him sliding into the seat beside her.

'Are you telling me that I have to keep my hands to myself?' he asked softly. 'I can't guarantee that I can, with you in that unbelievably tantalising dress.' His voice grew husky. 'I particularly like the way it drapes around your . . . curves.' His finger reached out to follow the line, and she steeled herself not to respond but to throw him a withering look. He chuckled and eyed her lazily. 'You are voluptuous. You look like a celebration of womanhood. And having those straps across one shoulder with the other one bare gives an impression of abandon.'

'You saw my luggage. This is the only dress that I could screw into a small space and that wouldn't need ironing,' she muttered, angry that her body had responded to his seductive tone.

'How practical,' he mocked gently. 'Yet, in that dress, with your hair tumbling over one eye, can you blame me if I make a pass?'

She hastily tucked her hair behind her ears. 'You men have got to realise that women dress up to please themselves, not to be alluring,' she chided.

'That explanation may fool Englishmen, but you forget I have hot Cretan blood running in my veins, Helen. I know when a woman wants to look good for a man by the way she eyes him. Let's be honest with each other about one thing, at least. Now I should tell you that normally I am slow to arouse and don't care for short-term relationships or casual girlfriends.' His voice grew throatier. 'But when I meet a woman who makes my stomach kick with desire and who both intrigues me and makes me laugh, then I'm not going to be put off, even if she pretends to fool herself and tries to fool me.'

'What—what do you mean?' she asked nervously.

'I know what's happening to you at this moment. I'm not blind. You feel the same primitive knives of physical need tearing into you as I do. So don't play coy. I prefer honesty from you.'

He switched on the engine and it throbbed like a husky tiger, adding to the sensuality in the air. The car moved smoothly away, leaving Helen in a state of turmoil. When he'd told her that he found her exciting, her heart had flipped over, then she'd remembered miserably that he couldn't be trusted. It devastated her that she'd been so transparent, since she'd thought her internal reactions had been rather well hidden! Worse still, he seemed pretty certain of himself and the outcome of the evening. Arrogant swine! She'd prove him wrong!

The Porsche was gloriously comfortable, the seat supporting her every curve, and it was exhilarating being in such a beautiful car. The sun cast long, fingering shadows along the valley, and then the sapphire sky became tinged with the palest pink which deepened to a fiery red. Cranes winged their homeward way over the mountains, silhouetted against the sunset.

Dimitri refrained from talking, letting the valley speak to Helen instead. She occasionally shared her pleasure with him, smiling shyly and receiving a gentle smile in return. As they drove along the main road, Dimitri put on a cassette of headily throbbing music. It wasn't long before it had seeped into Helen's bones, and she felt less sure of her abilities to resist him. He was a very clever man, she decided sadly, one who'd eat little girls like her for breakfast. They turned off the main road somewhere above the bay of Mirabello, and she saw with a start that there was a barrier across the road, similar to the one in Vronda valley.

Directly in front of Dimitri's Porsche was a hired car, and its driver was arguing with the two uniformed guards. Helen glanced curiously at the German shepherd dog by the barrier. The savage-looking beast was chewing a large bone with daunting ferocity.

'Do you think that's the remains of a guest who tried to

escape?' she asked.

Dimitri chuckled. 'It could be that he's sampling tonight's main course. Want to turn around.?' he asked lightly.

'Don't you dare to suggest such a thing!' Helen watched as the driver failed to persuade the guards to raise the barrier, and drove away looking very frustrated. 'Why wouldn't they let that man in, do you suppose?' she queried.

'Probably didn't have a reservation,' said Dimitri, turning to nod at one of the guards. *'Kalispera.'*

'Evening, sir.'

Helen was surprised. Why talk English to Dimitri when he was so obviously a Greek?

'Evening. I have booked a table.'

'Fine, sir. Have a pleasant evening.'

'Thank you.'

The barrier was lifted and they drove through lush gardens, softly lit by subtle floodlights.

'Is that all?'

'What?' Dimitri flicked a quick glance at her. 'I don't understand.'

'Two guards and a vicious-looking dog, and all they do is check you've booked? It doesn't make sense.'

'I think they also size up people. We obviously looked good enough for the Palace.'

'Snobs,' snorted Helen, settling back to enjoy the gardens.

The hotel entrance was intimidating. Two smartly dressed flunkeys leapt down to open the car doors, and Dimitri, perfectly used to opulence and service, casually handed over the car keys, taking Helen by the elbow and escorting her up the broad golden marble steps. There were men beside the automatic glass doors, too, welcoming them discreetly. Helen's eyes widened at the vast foyer which was glittering with mirrors and chandeliers and extravagant plants. In the centre, a small oasis of date palms had been landscaped around a tinkling fountain.

'I think I can see a Judas-tree! Can we go over?' she asked in awe, pointing to the centrepiece.

'Be my guest.' Dimitri smiled at something that had amused him and led her across the gleaming, bronze marble floor, his hand beneath her elbow. Helen sat on a low wall and trailed her fingers in the cascading stream, gasping with delight as golden carp sucked at her hand.

'I have to remember every bit of this,' she said enthusiastically.

The smile on Dimitri's face faded. 'Oh, why?'

'To tell my father, of course,' she said, engrossed in the extraordinary sensation of the little fishy mouths and happily ignorant of his stony expression. 'I wish I'd brought my notebook—I could have written things down and not forgotten anything. Do you think they have brochures with pictures?'

'Possibly,' said Dimitri, sounding bored.

Helen stood up, flushing. 'You must think I'm awfully naïve,' she said, with a little tilt of her chin. 'But I can't be blasé and pretend all this is normal to me, because I'm just not used to this kind of world. It's like a fairyland. We've always lived a very ordinary life, and this is way out of my league. You'll have to excuse me if I embarrass you, but I want to enjoy all this.'

'You don't embarrass me,' he said slowly. 'So many women are jaded with life, or think it is sophisticated to control their delight. I like the way you respond. Don't change, it's very refreshing and I enjoy your pleasure.'

She tucked her arm in his. 'You're a nice man underneath,' she declared, cocking her head up to look at him saucily.

'I'm not too thrilled or flattered with your choice of adjective, but it's probably the nearest thing to a compliment I'm likely to get from you,' he said drily. 'Now, the bar is over to the left. Would you like a drink before dinner?'

Of course, she realised, he would have been here before.
It was just his style—coolly formal and impersonal, slavering
servants and expensive dishes. No, that wasn't fair. He had
no pretensions, and no one had slavered yet!

'Yes, please,' she said. 'I want to see everything. Afterwards, can we wander around? That notice says there are
shops and saunas down there.'

'If you like.'

Helen grew thoughtful. He was saying all the right things,
but there was something wrong, as if he *was* disappointed.
He was being wary again, too. She gave an inward sigh.
She'd known they had nothing in common. Their worlds
were too far apart. Like ought to mix with like. At least
coming here had exposed the differences between them and
shown her that their worlds would never touch. So she might
as well make the best of it and enjoy the evening her way,
since it was definitely going to be the last time they went out
together!

Immediately they walked into the comfortable bar, she
noticed that the bar staff became unnaturally alert. Although
a couple sat down at the bar before they did, the head
barman came straight over to Dimitri. That was what
money and power did for you, she mused.

'Good evening, sir.'

'Evening. What would you like to drink, Helen?' asked
Dimitri.

'White wine, please, medium,' she said.

'And a Spritzer Kir for me,' he told the barman.

When their drinks arrived, he touched her glass with his.
'*Yasou,*' he smiled.

Embarrassed by the close attention of the barman, Helen
dropped her eyes and eagerly examined the room, frowning
in her effort to remember it all, her face intent. When she
turned back to Dimitri, she found that he too was scanning

the room, his face brooding and watchful. She wondered what he was looking for. Something to complain about?

'Well, do you like what you see?' he asked, seeing that she was staring at him.

'It's so difficult,' she complained, 'trying to photograph all this in my mind. And I haven't got round to the women's diamond-encrusted gowns yet!'

'Neither have I,' he said. 'I'm too busy looking at you.'

'Liar. You've been checking the talent—I've seen your eyes roaming!' she teased, a little hurt that he hadn't been concentrating completely on her.

Somewhere behind them, a waiter dropped his tray with a clang and two extraordinary things happened. Dimitri's dark eyes flashed a brief message of annoyance at the man, and at the same time Helen was aware that the eyes of every member of the staff there had swivelled nervously to gauge Dimitri's reaction.

'How extraordinary! These people are terrified of you!' she said in astonishment.

'Nonsense,' he retorted curtly. 'You're imagining things. What do you think of the pianist?'

Helen sipped her wine and frowned at the blatant change of subject. Well, she wouldn't push it now, but there was a decidedly odd atmosphere, as if everyone was on their toes.

'Wonderful. He has such a rich voice.' He was playing 'Yesterday,' one of her favourites, and she allowed herself to be diverted temporarily from asking Dimitri whether he'd been here before and perhaps complained about the service. Something had happened to create this tense atmosphere. The music flowed into her body and she swayed gently.

'Are those weavings on the bar ceiling from the village of Kritsa?' she asked. She'd heard that Kritsa was renowned for its woven goods, and wanted to go there.

'Yes, that's right.' Dimitri turned to the head barman.'What family made these?' he enquired.

'I don't know, sir. But . . . Hari!' He had snapped his fingers. 'Xaridhmos—Hari—is from Kritsa. He will know.' Helen saw how the tall, dark Cretan near the piano had jerked to attention and came hurrying over.

'Hair, this gentleman wishes to know who made the tapestries.'

'Yes, sir,' he said nervously. 'The family Lianis.'

Hari looked so petrified that Helen simply had to put him at his ease.

'Does each family have its own special design, then?' she asked with a smile.

'Yes, miss,' he said stiffly.

'Do any of your family weave?'

'Yes, miss. My mother and my aunt and my wife.'

'And your children, when they grow older, perhaps?' she said encouragingly.

Hari unbent a little. 'I have only a boy today. He is half-past two,' he said proudly.

'Half . . . oh! How lovely! Will I see your family working, and your little boy, if I go to Kritsa?' she asked, valiantly stifling her gurgling laughter. Half-past two!

He shot Dimitri a questioning look, and met only impassivity. 'I—yes, we are the first shop as you enter the village,' he said hesitantly.

'I'll make sure I go in and say hello,' she beamed. How nice these people were! Though Dimitri did make them edgy.

Hari bowed slightly and melted away. The music drifted romantically, leaving Helen quite sentimental. Her head tipped to one side as her dreamy eyes wandered, till she became aware that a powerful force was pulling her attention back to Dimitri.

'Helen——' His husky tones were cut off by the head barman.

'Excuse me, sir, there is a telephone call for you.'

'I'm not available. Tell them to call me tomorrow, please,' he said, his brows angry.

'It is urgent, sir.'

'It's all right,' said Helen. 'I'm quite happy here, listening and looking. You go ahead. Please.' She gave him a little push.

'Very well,' he said reluctantly. 'Order what you like and charge it up, all right? I won't be long.' He stood there, hesitating, and then bent and kissed her cheek.

Helen watched him stride easily across the room, watched by everyone. There was a noticeable relaxation in the tense staff, and Helen realised they'd been anxious ever since he'd walked in. Dimitri was apparently a man to be feared! Trust her to tangle with him!

Someone accidentally nudged her elbow and then apologised; it was the black American pianist, who had taken a break and was asking for a glass of water.

'Excuse me,' she said on impulse, 'I hope you don't mind me bothering you, but I love the way you sing. You have a marvellous voice. I know this isn't the done thing, but can I offer you a drink?'

'Well . . . sure, OK,' he said with a grin. 'Since I imagine Kastelli is paying. I'll have a lager and lime.'

'You know Dimitri?' she asked, interested.

'Know him?' He laughed. 'You don't know a man like that. He keeps himself strictly apart. Doesn't worry me, lady, as long as he pays my salary.'

'Yes, of course,' she said, hoping he'd say more. This was fascinating!

He took a long draught of lager. 'Thirsty work, singing, thanks a lot. You know, it must be one hell of a responsibility owning hotels, aware that thousands of people rely on you for their livelihood. Not to mention the strain of pleasing those demanding guests all over the world.'

'His . . . hotels? All over . . .' She gulped, beginning to

understand. 'How many are there, exactly?'

'I've played every one, little lady,' he said proudly. 'Must be fifteen. That doesn't sound a lot, but when you know they're the top fifteen in the world, that makes it sound different, eh?'

'Yes,' said Helen, despondent suddenly. 'It does.'

No wonder the staff were edgy. No wonder they acted oddly. He'd probably primed them not to acknowledge him. She remembered how he'd tried to make her change her mind about coming here. Oh, bother it! The distant, un-approachable landowner had turned into a creature from outer space as far as she was concerned! Well, now she knew that Dimitri and his father were two of the wealthiest men in the world, she hardly had a chance of fighting him about the Flower Walks. It was going to be all down to whether he liked her or not and trusted her.

Still, she sighed, it had helped to kill her physical longing for him. In any relationship a girl like her had with Dimitri Kastelli, she'd only get a bit part. He'd take the lead and walk off with the prizes. Of course, handling people was one of the skills of a hotel magnate. Personnel management was the essence of a successful business. He'd certainly handled her. Manipulated her, in fact.

Helen swilled the wine around in her glass gloomily.

'Known Kastelli long?' asked the singer.

'No, a few days.' Then why, she thought, was she so miserable at the realisation that the relationship would be short-lived? She had known he was a complex man, one who had a wide experience of life, a man who was making life serve him and not the other way around. She couldn't like someone who operated so ruthlessly.

'Must get back,' said the singer. 'Bye.'

Sadly she listened to 'You Are Beautiful'.

'I wish I could sing that to you,' said Dimitri softly in her ear.

'Cut that out!' she said crossly, gulping down her wine.

'My apologies. Shall we go in for dinner?'

Her big eyes, moist with tears, lifted to his. 'I—I don't think I want any,' she said in a small voice.

'Helen! What . . .' He looked around in irritation. 'Hell! Come with me. No, I insist. Everyone's looking at us. I can't talk to you here.'

His arm curled around her protectively and she wanted to lean into his body. Instead she walked very stiffly, stalking across the floor, suffering under the fascinated gazes of the guests and staff alike. Dimitri spoke rapidly in Greek to a man at the reception desk, and then led her down a small corridor.

'We can be private in here,' he said, eyeing her gently rolling tears in alarm. 'It's the manager's office. Apparently . . .'

'Don't tell me any more lies!' she cried, striding in angrily and confronting him. 'Why didn't you tell me who you were? I would have . . . I . . . Oh, damn you, damn you to hell!'

'What do you know about me, Helen?' he asked softly.

'I know you are immensely wealthy and *own* this hotel. And all the others that famous people go to! Why didn't you say? Were you afraid I'd latch on to you like a leech? Did you think I was a gold-digger? Do I look like a gold-digger?' she challenged.

'No,' he admitted. 'Nor do you behave like one. But . . . Helen, please sit down. This will take a little while.' He pressed a buzzer, and immediately there was a quiet knock on the door and one of the hotel staff entered.

'Andreos, please bring us a plate of smoked salmon, some fruit and coffee,' ordered Dimitri.

'Why do you speak English?' she asked sullenly.

'As a courtesy, so you understand what's going on,' he answered.

'That'll make a change.'

He bit his lip. 'You can't expect me to tell my life story to people I've only just met,' he said.

'You don't seem too slow to kiss them,' she accused.

'I *am* normally. You're different,' he growled. 'And I didn't lie, I just avoided telling you anything about myself.'

'*Why?*' It was the fact he didn't trust her or want to confide in her that hurt. Though, she acknowledged with a sigh, she was holding back on him too. They were both walking around each other in wary circles.

'Security. At this moment, my hotels all hold their usual assortment of famous people from the entertainment world, jet-setters, wealthy businessmen, Arab princes, kings, queens, heads of state . . .'

'I get the picture,' Helen sighed. 'You're incredibly important.'

'Dammit, that's not what I was getting at! Listen!' he said irritably. He began to lope around the room restlessly, unable to settle. She watched from the deep armchair, and wondered how such a young man could control the huge empire. He must be exceptionally talented.

'Helen, all those people live under threats to their lives. It's part of my job to protect them. That's why people like that use my hotels: they're the safest in the world. No one, but no one gets into the grounds without the staff being absolutely certain that they are what they say they are. I wasn't sure if you knew who I was and preferred you not to know.'

'You can't have suspected me! I'm not like terrorists or abductors, or . . .'

'You had binoculars, a camera, a notebook and you asked questions. My instincts told me you were innocent, that nobody could be as naïve as you and so obvious . . .'

'Thanks.'

'You're welcome,' he smiled wryly, pausing while their

simple supper was brought in. 'But, you see, it's perfectly possible that you were set up by a boyfriend—given some story about holiday walks, whereas in truth he was using you to find a way to crack my security. It happens, you know.'

'Me? A gangster's moll?' Helen looked affronted and Dimitri laughed, watching as she began to devour the smoked salmon.

'It sounds ridiculously dramatic, but that's the kind of world I live in,' he insisted. 'You seemed to be fitting the pattern. All this talk about remembering every bit of the hotel to tell your father . . .'

'That's the truth! He saved up all his club money so that I could splash out on a restaurant meal while I was over here,' said Helen quietly. 'Every Saturday since I can remember, he went to the club and had a pint, played snooker and had a game of darts. He loved it. For three months he didn't go, and I thought it was because Mum had died. But he was depriving himself so he could save that money for me. And I was going to tell him what a wonderful place I went to, and . . .' her voice filled with tears ' . . . and what a wonderful time I had, so he would think his sacrifice was w-w-worth while!'

'Hey, sweetheart,' said Dimitri gently, kneeling by her chair and taking her in his arms. 'I believe you. Yet I had to protect the lives of all those people, Helen. Do you understand? I don't always like what I have to do, but it takes some guts to run a place like this. If I could only go back to the day I first saw you . . .'

'You drove right past!' she mumbled into his shoulder.

'I had to warn the guard to turn you back and tell him what to say. I thought I'd better not get involved. But now I am, deeply involved.'

He tipped up her chin and looked seriously into her dark, brimming eyes.

'*Don't!*' she cried, pushing him away, her face full of fear.

She was poised to make a fool of herself.

'But . . .'

'Don't!'

Silently Dimitri rose, stood looking at her for a few seconds while she studied her hands in her lap, and then he walked over to the french windows, staring out intently.

'Would you like me to arrange for someone else to drive you back?' he asked in a cold, remote tone.

Helen's heart froze. 'I've offended you,' she whispered.

'Yes. You invited me with your eyes and body, and then rejected me. I don't like that kind of behaviour. I don't like being made a fool of,' he said tightly.

It was best this way, she thought dully. There was no point in letting him play squire and peasant girl with her, it would only end in misery.

She considered his offer. Paying for a taxi or engaging one of his staff to drive her to Vronda would be peanuts to a man like him.

'I have an alternative suggestion,' he said, facing her. 'Instead of going back to the cottage, you can stay here as long as you like. Alone, of course.'

'I'd look great, coming down to breakfast in my slinky Grecian number,' she said bitterly.

'I could send a man for your things.'

'Even better,' she said scornfully. 'Little shorts, T-shirts and walking-boots.'

'Sorry, I forgot. Look . . . there doesn't seem much point in staying in Crete. Why don't you go home, Helen? Back to England, where you belong?'

'I have to stay,' she said stubbornly, her heart lurching at his stony face. 'I have a job to do.'

'My God!' he roared. 'You're not still intending to go ahead with that stupid idea about botanists and . . .'

'It's *not* stupid!' she cried. 'I'll go and talk to your father and mother. Maybe they'd listen to me.'

Dimitri hauled her up out of the chair and shook her, his eyes blazing. 'I will not have my parents or myself—or any member of my staff—put in jeopardy because some curvy little blonde wants to prove a point,' he seethed. 'The reputation of the Kastelli security is at stake. If the public began to wander around the gorge, then my safety precautions would be impossible to maintain.'

'Why on earth would anyone want to abduct you?' she asked scornfully.

'There are several reasons,' he snapped. 'Anyone in my family could be held to ransom. It's been tried before. Or terrorists might try to reach heads of state through me. I know all the projected holiday venues, security procedures and so on. I have a key to every door in every hotel and also to every safe. Incidentally, by telling you this, you realise that I am chancing my arm about your innocence.'

'I'm not a threat to you,' she quavered.

'No? That remains to be seen,' he frowned. 'Helen, I stand firm about your plans. Find another valley. Find another gorge. There are thousands of them in Crete. I could get you free accommodation almost anywhere you chose. Take the offer. It's all you'll get. Persist in this mad scheme of yours and I'll fight you. Remember this, Helen: I am a Cretan. I am a Kastelli. You'll meet no more formidable combination than that!'

Helen didn't like his merciless tone. He had the ability to switch from charm to steely determination. 'You are paranoiac. Maybe I'll use Vronda, maybe I shan't. But I told you before, I won't be pushed around or ordered to do anything by you. I wish to find out for myself what the situation is. Besides, Vronda has to be my base. I couldn't take your charity. I can live in that house rent-free, you see. That means a lot to someone as poor as I am,' she added proudly.

'All right,' he growled, hauling her closer. 'Let's see how

how poor you are. Let's see how much you care for the welfare of your father. Agree to forget the idea of the walks, agree to leave and never return, and I'll pay you off handsomely. Another thing: give me Maria's address, so I can make an offer for her house and land.'

He released her and drew a cheque-book from his pocket. 'Here,' he said, tearing off a cheque and showing her what he had written. 'Your hush money. That would help your father, wouldn't it?'

Helen gasped at the amount and sat down suddenly. Misery tore at her breast to discover that her fears were true: all he wanted was to make the whole of Vronda his own private playground. He dealt in money and possessions, and wielded emotion as a weapon. He was a callous swine to have treated her in such a cavalier fashion!

'I am not to be bought off! My father and I have more honour than you. I'll tell you this: I *will* succeed in my plans and that house will never become yours. Please arrange a taxi for me. I never want to see you or speak to you again. You have insulted me and I despise your mercenary, coldblooded behaviour.'

The black fury on Dimitri's face terrified her. For a moment, she thought he was going to say something. His body quivered with barely controlled passion. Then he made a curt phone call and strode out. Helen curled up in the armchair and tried to stop her own body shaking. In the short time she had known him, Dimitri had confused, exhilarated and distressed her. He had made her experience a sensuality that shocked her, and a hatred that bewildered her.

But there was no doubt that she was even more determined about the walks than before. Vronda would become her holiday base. She'd get the villagers on her side somehow, and show Dimitri Kastelli that there were other ways of achieving success than by bullying tactics.

On the way back, Helen was silent, planning what she

would do. She lay in bed, thinking, willing herself to wake
early. Tomorrow she would walk the gorge, and to hell with
the consequences!

CHAPTER SEVEN

IT WAS a wonderful morning. The larks were already busily filling the air with soaring song when Helen began to walk along the *kalderim,* and green and indigo dragonflies darted like vivid jewels among the wild lupins.

Helen felt saturated in sunlight. It heated through the thin cotton of her short-sleeved shirt so that her skin glowed with warmth. She stopped to photograph a particularly striking carob tree, its long, green pods dangling beneath the dark, glossy leaves. There were beautiful views in all directions, and Helen was determined to make this one of the Walks. With any luck, the gorge would be interesting too, and could be included as a contrast to the lush valley.

As she neared the gorge entrance where the rock rose dramatically to tower over the narrow gap, she searched the hills with her binoculars to see whether anyone was spying on her. Apart from distant sounds of workers in the fields, she was alone and unobserved. Not that it mattered, of course, she was well within her rights.

With a nervous feeling in her stomach, however, she left the paved road and plunged through the dense undergrowth which covered a narrow path leading between the great cliffs. Slowly, taking in her surroundings, she walked alongside the bleached white pebble bed of the rushing river and came out into another world.

The gorge was wider than she'd originally thought from studying the map. Sheer limestone cliffs supported a surprising variety of trees: cypress, pine, holm oak, cedar—all somehow rooted in impossible crevices. There were caves, too, which would yield interesting specimens. Helen decided not to make detailed investigations at this moment, but to concentrate on the route.

The beauty, the grandeur of the ravine was breaktaking. Time and time again, as she walked in the glorious sunshine, she found herself wishing someone was with her so that she could exclaim aloud and share her excitement. She remembered then that Dimitri had said it was dark and cold. What a liar he was! But recalling his untrustworthy behaviour soured her thoughts for a moment, and she took a nut bar from her pocket to munch and cheer herself up.

The ravine twisted and turned in snake-like coils, meandering so tightly that there was a different view around every bend. At one point, the fast-flowing river was forced to tumble through a narrow gap. The wide track that was probably the route Dimitri took to his house disappeared in a tunnel hewn in the rock, and all the donkey paths converged on it. It was Helen's only way through.

She could tell from the brilliant sunlight at the other end that the ravine widened again, but she wasn't prepared for the sight that met her eyes. High on a ledge, in solitary splendour above a tortuous road, was a house. No, she corrected in her mind, a palace. King Minos's Palace.

It was huge, built on the lines of a Greek temple, appearing to grow out of rock and soil. Elegant Grecian pillars and arcades supported gently sloping roofs with cinnamon-coloured hoop tiles. The graceful, classical lines of the building subtly hid the fact that it was modern, and that its multitude of terraces had been recently constructed. Helen admired the great sweeps of purple bougainvillaea and, through her binoculars, could just make out huge white lilies clustered thickly by tall Ali Baba pots edging the terraces.

Suddenly, dogs began to bark and she shrank back into the tunnel. A dark figure appeared. Even at that distance Helen found no difficulty in identifying Dimitri's fine physique. He yelled at the dogs and scanned the gorge, then ordered the dogs inside with him.

Hesitantly she looked out, and then dashed along the track, hoping she couldn't be seen, wending her way through thick undergrowth until she could turn off on to a small path that led upwards. For a long time she walked, enjoying the scent of the herbs as she brushed against them, the Jerusalem sage particularly strong here and a magnet for huge bumble bees. Then something high in a little crack in the cliff above attracted her eye. It could possibly be the rare and insignificant little Dittany plant that she'd been looking for. She had to find out! Feeling very excited, Helen carefully laid down her pack and scanned the cliff with a practised eye.

It didn't look too difficult. Her small feet took her safely and surely up, till she was about twenty feet from the ground. She paused and stared at the plant, holding herself very still. The Dittany—for that was what it was—had tucked itself in a minute fissure on the rockface.

'Don't move.'

Helen froze to hear the soft, warning voice. Oh, God! What was Dimitri going to do? She was at his mercy here. She gripped the rock face in terror. He could . . .

'Hold on, I'm coming.'

She turned around, petrified.

'Helen!' he called in alarm. 'Don't look down! Just hang on and I'll be there!'

In utter relief at her stupid imagination, she held on to the cliff and giggled.

'Now, don't get hysterical,' he said in a calming tone, trying to find suitable footholds. 'Everything's all right. I'll get you down in a moment.'

'I don't want to get down, you interfering idiot!' she gurgled. 'I'm on my way up. I don't need your help. I'm probably a better climber than you.'

He drew level with her and gaped at her amused gaze, then an angry flush appeared on his face.

'You'd frozen. You'd panicked . . .'

'Rubbish,' she laughed, moving up easily to examine more closely the little heart-shaped leaves of the plant and ignoring him. Yet the spark had still been there between them. It had leapt in her heart to see the concern on his face.

'Oh, my God!' he breathed.

Helen heard him making his way down, and she decided she couldn't stay up there much longer. But when she reached the ground and turned to make a scathing comment, she found him with his back to her and gripping the trunk of a tree as if his very life depended on it.

She felt terribly contrite. He had been trying to save her, after all.

'Dimitri . . .'

'Don't do that to me again,' he said savagely. He whirled around and his eyes blazed with fire. 'I thought you were stuck. I thought you might fall! God, Helen, you could have broken your silly little neck! Have you no thought for other people? Don't you care that . . .' He broke off, his chest heaving with indignation. 'Curse you,' he muttered, coming straight for her.

'No, Dimitri, it wasn't my fault that you . . .'

He caught hold of her and drew her to him, ignoring her protests, a dangerous look on his face as if he intended to do exactly as he liked.

'I was so afraid for you,' he muttered as his lips ranged her upturned, astonished face.

'No, Dimitri.' She struggled.

'God, I must be mad!' he groaned. 'You're causing me so much trouble; every hour you're in Vronda I gain two more grey hairs.'

There was a silence as his mouth swept across hers and passionately savoured its soft fullness. Helen felt herself sinking into his arms, unable to prevent herself from responding as his lips took rougher possession. Then he pulled away and looked at her, anger and desire mingled in his expression.

'You threaten my reputation——'

'You threaten mine,' she muttered huskily.

His mouth descended again, this time skilfully parting her lips, and a bolt of desire rocketed through her body as his tongue erotically explored, teased, tantalised and promised.

With a throaty moan, his head jerked back and Helen could see that he was trying to control himself.

'I saw you——' he began.

Helen heart thudded. 'You were spying on me!' she cried unhappily.

'Watching,' he growled. 'One of my men told me you were on the track up here. I set out to make sure you were all right. When I saw you clambering up that rock, as if you had no concept of safety . . .'

'It's a simple climb!' she cried heatedly, wishing he'd release her. The heat of their bodies was sending her crazy.

'I didn't know you were *that* experienced,' he snapped. 'You don't look . . .' His eyes dropped to her rapidly rising breasts and hung there, avid with hunger. 'You look far too . . .' His husky voice died away, his gaze saying it all.

'I can't help my shape,' she croaked.

'No,' he murmured, taking a firmer hold on her back with one hand. The other reached out and Helen watched, mesmerised, as his long fingers stretched out.

Her throat had dried completely and all her body waited for his touch. With a supreme effort she gritted her teeth.

'Don't you dare touch me,' she grated, anger at her own stupid, traitorous body flaring in her eyes.

'Hell!' Dimitri's hands dropped to his sides. His body trembled with barely controlled desire. Then his superb self-discipline mastered his primitive needs, and he moved away, thrusting his hands in his pockets and scowling at her ferociously.

'I don't *want* to want you,' he muttered.

'Thanks,' she said bitterly. 'It bothers you, does it? You don't like the idea of mixing with the peasants?'

'Don't be ridiculous! I don't give a damn how much money you've got in the bank, or who sired you! You, lady, have one hell of a chip on your shoulder!'

'No, I——' She stopped. 'Yes, you're right,' she corrected. 'I had no idea until I met you that there could be such a gulf between the rich and the poor. I thought there was no difference between people, that the wealthy were only ordinary human beings with more money. There's something else, though, isn't there? We live in different worlds with different values and aims. I want to give pleasure to people who enjoy the simple, natural world. You scheme and plot and fight a battle every day of your life to protect a small minority of people who are terrified to exist.'

'That's not fair!'

'You're damn right it isn't fair!' she yelled, thumping her hands on to her hips, incensed. 'But that's how the world works. I'm sorry I crept in under your defences,' she said, tilting her head defiantly and making sure he knew she intended a double meaning. 'But that's your problem, not mine. I suggest you keep out of my way. I'm liable to get violent if you persecute me any more.'

'Persecute!' he roared. 'You're persecuting *me*! Yesterday I was in the middle of an emergency meeting in Athens and my mind drifted off, thinking of you in those ridiculous little shorts and those boots that look too heavy for your little feet! Then at lunch, I found myself meandering again with nothing but an image of your incredibly sensual lips as you ate that orange when we had breakfast. You're driving me out of my mind!'

Helen stared at him, aghast, and shrank back against the

cliff. 'I don't want . . .'

'I know,' he said grimly. 'Neither do I. I'm a sensible, serious, controlled man, always controlled unless I choose to show anger. I've never been so damned excitable before, and it's all due to you and the effect you have on my senses! Other women come and go in my life without disturbing much more than the surface. You, you wretched voluptuary, are destroying my concentration! When I'm not with you I'm restless, as if something's missing. When I am with you, I'm alternately infuriated and entranced. I'm going haywire, Helen, and I will not have that!'

She closed her eyes to shut out the sight of him. All she wanted to do was to run into his arms and tell him that she felt the same, that no matter what their differences were she had a terrible sensation of destiny when he was with her, as if they were both meant for each other.

'Try calling up an old girlfriend,' she suggested, her voice uneven.

Pains lashed through her body at the idea of him making love to another woman. Jealousy! She'd never been jealous—never needed to be. Her cruel imagination flashed a vision into her head of Dimitri and a sultry beauty naked on an enormous bed before she could stop it.

'I want you,' he growled huskily, and Helen read the intention in his eyes. She began to run, but his long legs caught her easily and she was pushed against the rock.

'I want you,' he murmured seductively. 'I have to hold you, to touch, to kiss you. Every second we're apart I'm only half a person, Helen.'

His body pressed firmly against hers and her pulses raced at the hard, unyielding muscles and the sensation of over-powering masculinity that emanated from him. He wanted her and he was determined to have her. He had the strength and the will-power, and probably the ruthlessness, to take her. More than that: he had her own sexuality on his side!

'Please don't,' she mumbled miserably.

'Live dangerously, surrender, experiment. We both know
it's inevitable,' he said throatily. 'Why be so hesitant? Let
me show you what it can be like between us. Let me give you
pleasure. I want to give you pleasure, Helen. Give yourself
up to me and enjoy yourself.'

His soft breath fanned her face and made her quiver. It
seemed that he was arousing all her senses and numbing her
brain. Bewildered, she tried to gather her thoughts together,
and failed. His mouth was sliding with the most exquisite
precision over every centimetre of her throat.

'Helen!' he whispered, his voice shaking with intensity.

She moaned. They stared into each other's eyes for a
moment and then she watched his lashes flutter down in
sheer pleasure and the sultry curve of his mouth moved
nearer and nearer to her trembling lips.

'No,' she protested. 'You . . . I don't . . . like . . . you!'

'That's all right,' he crooned. 'I'll settle for lust.'

'Well, I won't!' she wailed.

He laughed gently, and she melted as his lips moved over
hers. Subtly his tongue slipped into her mouth, and they
both gasped together at the violent spasms of hungry desire
that his action aroused. He slowly moved his hands up from
her waist to her breasts, and lightly circled them with his
forefingers.

'No, it's . . . it's too soon, I——' She bit her lip at the
exquisite sensation.

'I know it's too soon. It's completely impossible that I
should want you so much and miss you when you're not
around. There's no way that you could have established
yourself so firmly in my mind and aroused me so deeply.
But you have. My God, you have!'

He kissed her sweetly, stroking her shaking body, thrilling
every nerve with the slow seduction of his mouth, his voice
and his skilful touch. Gently he slipped her top

button from its buttonhole and allowed his mouth to trail over her collarbone and down, down, his fingers quickly undoing her other buttons until he was pushing aside the delicate lace of her bra and his fingers had found at last the violently throbbing peaks of her breasts.

Helen couldn't move. All she wanted was for the pleasure to go on and on. And then his head bent and, for the first time in her life, she felt the warm moistness of a man's mouth tugging at her breast and was unable to contain her need any longer

Her hands dug deeply into his shoulders with the sweet pain as she rocked on her heels from the intensity of her emotions, hardly able to stand because her knees seemed to want to buckle and her body was preparing to collapse to the ground.

'Helen!'

She moaned at the intensity of his whisper. It came from deep inside him and, in her impassioned state, seemed to be a cry of longing that was more than sex itself. I'm fooling myself, she thought. I want him to feel more for me than naked hunger, and I'm allowing my fantasy to take over.

'Let me make love to you,' he murmured, lifting his head, his strong hands supporting her tiny, trembling body.

Lust, he'd said. He would settle for lust. He cared nothing for love, the real reason two lovers gave themselves to each other. He wanted her body and pure physical pleasure. She wanted that too, but much, much more. The fact that such needs didn't even enter his mind filled her with dismay. They were on two different planes in that as well, then, she thought with sorrow.

'Let me,' he coaxed, gently teasing her lips with his tongue.

'*No!*' she breathed vehemently, wincing at the shocked agony in his eyes.

'God! You can't do this to me!' he groaned.

She stopped him, just as he was about to claim her mouth. 'That's enough!' she rapped, panic in her voice. What was she more afraid of? she wondered. Him? Or the way she would almost certainly surrender unconditionally if he went one step further?

'Helen, I——' He took one look at her frightened face and let out a harsh, rasping breath. Slowly his hands released her and he walked away.

'Will you please go?' she asked shakily.

'In a minute.' He was fighting for control. 'Look . . . it's no good trying to pretend this hasn't happened, or that you didn't like what I was doing. Oh, I know that's not the gentlemanly thing to say, but I deal in realities. Tell me honestly, Helen. Do you hate me, despise me? Do you want me to go right out of your life?'

She dropped her lashes to cover her eyes, knowing she couldn't answer.

Dimitri heaved a huge sigh. 'I seem to have bungled this,' he muttered. 'You see, something about you makes me forget my calm, well-ordered way of behaving, and I turn into a . . .'

'An ordinary human being,' she finished, smiling at him wryly. It was funny, really, seeing him so confused.

He grinned and tousled his hair. 'I'm not used to feeling my control slipping away,' he said. 'It's damned disconcerting.'

She couldn't help a look of longing flash into her eyes at his bewildered face. Suddenly he seemed less intimidating and very, very appealing. Dimitri read her expression with growing hope.

'Helen . . . I wonder if you would mind starting again? Could we go back to the beginning of our relationship? You're obviously going to be around, getting in my hair, for a little while, and as sure as hell I'm going to be getting in yours! How about making a fresh start?'

'I don't know . . .'

'Please. We could try being polite to each other. There's no harm in that. We might even form a friendship.'

'I didn't think that was what you were after,' she said drily.

'It's the boots. I find them intensely erotic,' he admitted.

She roared with laughter, throwing her head back, suddenly elated. Perhaps if they took things more slowly, and at less of a gallop, they could make their relationship work. Deep inside her she knew there was something very special about the way she felt for him. She couldn't let him go, she'd regret it for ever more. Besides, she'd never get a wink of sleep all the time she was in Crete if they kept apart!

'Try fixing your eyes on my knees,' she suggested. 'No one could get excited about knees.'

'I'll do my best,' he said solemnly. 'Does that mean . . .'

'Dimitri,' she said frankly, 'I like you. Heaven knows why, because you don't deserve it at all.' She giggled at his hurt expression. 'You've either been perfectly discouraging or too encouraging. You need to get the balance right,' she said reprovingly.

'I'm sure if I topple over to one side you'll give me a hefty shove back,' he murmured, his eyes smiling. 'So. Friends?'

He held out a hand and she took it, laughing and following his eyes as they travelled to her feet, whereupon he shuddered with feigned passion and controlled himself theatrically. Then she looked down again, her eyes caught by a scattering of colour.

'Dimitri!' She crouched by some picked flowers, strewn on the ground.

'Oh, yes.' He sounded embarrassed. 'Just a few flowers I thought you might be interested in. Shall we . . .'

'Interested? I'll say! You shouldn't have dropped them like this.'

'You were stuck up a cliff, remember? I was doing my

hero bit. Let's go . . .'

'Dimitri,' she said breathlessly, collecting up each delicate stem. 'This one is rare—and this—and . . . I don't recognise these. They must be very unusual. Where did you find them?'

She looked up to find him staring down at her in a very perplexed way.

'Oh, there's lots of them around. I picked them as I went along,' he said causally.

'Where?' she insisted, jumping up. 'Show me!'

'Well, I can't now . . .'

'You're not going to start dissembling again!' she accused.

'I do have other things to do, Helen, besides grubbing in the grass for orchids,' he reminded her gently.

'You know what they are, then. You know they're unusual!'

'Well, yes. I'll tell you what,' he said slowly. 'To show we trust each other, why don't you come out with me tomorrow, and I go out with you the next day? I have to run over to the island in the bay, and you could come too. I'll bring a picnic. Then I can show you where a number of these orchids grow, high up at the top of the gorge. You'd love the walk there, it's fantastic,' he said enthusiastically.

'You always seem to bargain,' she commented, a little uncertainly. 'You scratch my back and I'll scratch yours kind of arrangement.'

'Sounds a good idea to me,' he smiled. 'Scratching backs, I mean. All right, only a joke! What about it?'

Helen looked at him doubtfully.

'On the boat we can both be ordinary people. We'll be on non-controversial grounds,' he coaxed in his velvet voice. 'I'll take the caique if you like, and we can sail over. It would mean an early start. I'd pick you up and drive you through the mountain pass up there'. His hand waved beyond his house, beyond the mountain range that hid them from the sea. 'There's a marvellous view of the bay. It's totally private, except for the fishermen, and we can swim there. Or we can swim on the island if you prefer. You'll like the island, it has a small colony of *agrimi*.'

'Chamois?' she asked, excited. 'Those goats with huge curling horns?'

'That's right,' he beamed. 'They're very shy and will only come out at dusk, but we can try to spot them. I'll pick you up at seven-thirty, shall I?'

CHAPTER EIGHT

THE SUN burnt deeply into Helen's tightly shut eyes. This was the hottest day since she'd arrived on Crete. Apart from the small area covered by her minute bikini, she was turning a deep golden colour, and after the cold spring in England— and the first day of her arrival—it was wonderful to feel warm through and through. She relaxed all her limbs with a little wriggle and sighed happily. They hadn't seen any of the rare wild goats, but the day had still been unforgettable. Dimitri had behaved perfectly, so that their relationship had been much more relaxed and friendly, though there had been times when Helen wished with a sudden irrationality that he would show some interest in her!

Knowing how minuscule her bikini was, she had chosen a prim blue sundress to wear on top, intending to put it on if Dimitri tried to take advantage of her and thought the bikini was her way of encouraging him. In actual fact, she'd packed for lightness and was wishing she'd put in her more demure one-piece. But it couldn't be helped, and perhaps it would be a good test of his intentions!

She'd twisted her hair into a knot on top of her head too, thinking that made her look a little more sophisticated than a diminutive young woman sporting a plait!

When they had crested the mountain pass and begun the tortuous climb down to the beach, Helen's breath had caught at the spectacular scene. Below was a beach of bleached white sand fringed with palm trees. It curved around to a narrow spit of land which thrust a finger of rock into the sea and then swelled into a little humped island. The

110

shimmering Aegean sea changed constantly under her sparkling eyes: sometimes it was turquoise, sometimes an iridescent peacock green. Further out to sea, and also in the shadow of the Greek fishing-smack bobbing by a tiny jetty, the sea had taken on the colour of a deep royal blue.

'Paradise Bay,' smiled Dimitri at her excited face.

And paradise it was. They carried a picnic hamper across the warm sand, making for the jetty, but Helen seemed to be constantly dropping her side of the hamper and begging him to stop so she could drink in the view.

'I keep expecting to see dusky maidens handing out Bounty bars,' she giggled, eyeing the palm trees, which were bending in a very photogenic manner over the sands.

Dimitri's grin made her heart lurch. 'You would have done last year. Someone twisted my father's arm one day, and he allowed them to come here to make advertising films.'

'Would you mind if I took a picture of the beach?' she asked hesitantly. Then a wicked look came into her eyes. 'There aren't any heads of state or important secret installations in the background that I can see.'

'Don't make fun of me, you saucy wench. Go ahead.'

'With you in it,' she begged. She'd have a picture of him to remember, if little else.

He frowned. 'If you don't mind, I'll push on and get the boat ready.'

'You don't really trust me, do you?' she said quietly.

'It's . . . let's say I'm very camera-shy.'

He walked off with a grin and a wave, but Helen was disappointed. He was a very cautious man. Ultra-cautious. She heaved a sigh, acknowledging that security and suspicion must be ingrained in him. His care for his guests was admirable. But she was different! He ought to trust her. She wouldn't go showing the picture to dozens of people and blabbing about him. She only wanted a memory that was more tangible than feelings of regret.

As she focused her camera, she heard the sound of a helicopter. She shot a glance at Dimitri and he was checking his watch. From the way he did it, it looked as if he knew it would be visiting the gorge. His dark eyes flashed warily in her direction, and he gave a start to see her looking at him.

'Someone for you?' she called.

'No. I expect my mother's going shopping.'

Helen didn't have a chance to respond to that because he strode off quickly. Shopping? How the rich did live!

Once on board, she forgot his reticence and her own doubts, as he quickly enlisted her as bosun and slave. She was so busy dashing about pulling every rope he pointed to and helping him to set the sails, that she didn't have time to think, and that suited her very well. Today, she decided, she would live for the moment.

They'd landed on the little island and she'd happily explored with him, scrambling over a ruined Venetian fortress that had once been captured by Barbarossa, the sixteenth-century Turkish pirate. Then he had taken her to a tiny, whitewashed oratory. Here he'd made notes and explained to her that he was checking on the work that needed to be done before Easter. Everything had to be freshly painted and in perfect order before the festival.

When he'd finished, Dimitri had led her to a perfect crescent of white sand, and they'd been there ever since lunch, lazing, talking and swimming in the glorious warm water of the shallow lagoon. Looking like a Greek god with his perfect physique, deep tan and confident air, and wearing only a pair of small black swimming trunks, he unbent in the drowsy sunshine and told her a great deal about his family.

'What does your father do all day?' she asked, idly sifting sand through her fingers. 'Can he be driven down here? Can he still enjoy the valley?'

'Yes, he likes to be driven about,' answered Dimitri, lying back with his arms under his head. 'I bring him down occasionally, and he takes a swim in the high summer when the water temperature is warmer.'

'It's an idyllic spot. You must have had lots of wonderful family picnics here,' she said enviously.

He gave a short, mirthless laugh. 'Us? None.'

'But——'

'Helen, my family isn't like yours. You must understand that my mother loves only my father, he loves only the business, and up to now I've loved nothing apart from Vronda.' His mouth twisted at Helen's horrified face. 'People can get along without family affection,' he said quietly. 'I've done so all my life.'

'That's no recommendation,' she grinned. 'But . . . I don't understand your parents' attitude. Surely they must love you!'

'You do live in an unreal world, don't you?' he said gently. 'I suppose for someone like you, who's been wrapped in love, given and received it all your life, it must be difficult to understand the behaviour and motives of warring families.'

'Didn't you ever share special moments?' she asked, aghast. He was right, it was something she couldn't imagine.

'Not that I can remember,' he said laconically. 'My parents don't do things together. They certainly don't include me in their plans. Mother always made sure I never entered my father's life and became a threat to her. I'm seen as the continuation of the Kastelli line, and someone who will make the business live for another generation. We are polite to each other and I am dutiful. That's about it.'

'How can you live without people loving you? How can you live without loving people?' she puzzled. 'Surely every baby is appealing? Or were you an awful child?'

He smiled wanly. 'Isolated. Until I went to school in Athens I had nannies and tutors. Father spent every waking hour working and was hardly home. Mother entertained. I walked the mountains during my holidays, and later I often didn't bother to come home from school. But I missed Vronda. This place is in my blood, you see. My family have been here for centuries, always running the taverna, handing it on father to son, father to son for generations. Sometimes I wonder what would have happened if my parents hadn't met.'

'You'd be serving me Greek coffee in Vronda and eyeing my shorts,' she said, trying to make him smile.

'To hell with the shorts, I've found something much more interesting to look at,' he grinned, ogling her breasts.

'Down boy, it's too hot,' she reproved, wanting to get him talking about himself again. It was helping her to understand how he ticked and explained a great deal. 'Your parents must have loved each other to begin with,' she said, wriggling around to face Dimitri.

'Mother certainly fell for him; he was probably dazzled by her at first. To an ordinary village man she must have seemed very much a woman of the world, elegant and sophisticated. When he found that she was wealthy, he vowed to marry her and make her empire his. The custom on marriage is for the woman to sign over her worldly goods to her husband, you see. I think Father allowed his excitement about the contract to show. Mother's been very bitter ever since.'

'I'd hate not to have a loving father,' she said sympathetically.

'You're very lucky. But then, anyone would dote on you,' he smiled. 'Besides, don't feel too sorry for me. I have one or two things which compensate.'

'Swiss bank accounts?' she laughed.

'No. I enjoy the work and I am ecstatic about living here,'

he said softly.

'Then you can't be as bad as you seem,' she grinned.
'Even if you need a helicopter to go shopping! Oh, how
odd.' Her brow wrinkled. 'We heard it arrive to pick your
mother up, but we didn't hear it take off again.'

'You probably had your head wrapped up in the sail at
the time,' he said lightly, reminding her of the muddle she'd
got into at one stage.

'Probably! As a sailor, I'd make a good postman! When
were you planning on going back?' she asked. 'Have I time
for another swim?'

'I think so. Race you!'

He hurtled off over the sand, reaching the water and
cleaving it with a perfect dive before she had hardly got
started. They fooled around in the cooling silken sea for
ages, and Helen's heart thudded crazily to see him so happy.

'I'm going in!' she called, taking heed of the warning
signs. It was time she got home before she lost her head.

He strode over to take her hand, and they walked back.
Helen trembled slightly at his touch. There was something
different in the way she was feeling towards him now.

She kept her head lowered, watching the way the sand
moved over her toes as she walked. From under her lashes,
his long, tightly muscled legs, darkly tanned, filled her
vision. Suddenly she was uncomfortably aware of his body,
close to hers, its exuberant masculinity intensified by his
elated state. She lifted her head slightly to admire him, and
noticed a small mole on his left bicep. A ridiculous feeling of
affection flooded through her, for no reason at all that she
could see.

He looked down at her with quiet, steady eyes, and she
felt her body quiver. His face no longer seemed hard, cold or
aloof. It was as if she knew him very well—had known him
all her life—and as if they had begun to understand each
other in the way that close friends always did. Confused, she

hurried on, but he held her back, standing rock-still and forcing her to a halt.

Helen wouldn't look at him. A silent, inner strength and peace was flowing from him, and it was too magnetic for her to cope with. Every part of his being was pulling her towards him, not only physically, but more overwhelmingly in a mental and emotional way as well. In her heightened state, she imagined something deep inside him was calling her, and the longer she remained inactive, the less able she would be to resist that call.

Still he didn't speak, knowing instinctively, perhaps, that words would break the spell he'd woven between them. Instead, his hand reached out and lightly caressed her cheek. It was a small, insignificant gesture, but it was enough. He was waiting.

Why shouldn't she respond? Why not give in? That's what she wanted, after all. The battle within her showed plainly on her face, and still Dimitri waited. His silence, his sensitivity in allowing her to decide how their relationship should develop, touched her. She knew how her body was flushing and blooming for him. She knew how her breasts had firmed and that her nipples pressed in tight, peaking buds against her black bikini top. She knew that she'd found it impossible not to wriggle her thighs to dissipate the slowly rising heat there. All this he must have observed. With all his experience and mastery it would have been easy to seduce her, the state she was in.

And he was highly aroused, too. His chest was showing how heavily he was breathing; there was an erratic pulse beating in his throat, and the hand that stroked her face was shaking. Helen didn't dare to let her eyes wander below his waist, but knew that he must be showing evidence of his need for her. Despite his desire, he waited, telling her with every fibre of his being that he was there if she wanted him. It must be more difficult for him, she thought hazily, because he knew what sex was like; she didn't.

Nor must she know what it was like with him, now, on this beach. Oh, God! she groaned to herself, closing her eyes to banish him from her sight. Was this part of her Greek heritage, to be instantly aroused by a man she hardly knew? Now that she'd acknowledged her Mediterranean blood, had her mind thrown her into the deep well of passion? She couldn't be so stupid, so irrational!

Everything Liz and her father had taught her was against sex without marriage. She had grown up with a high level of morality which was prompted by concern and consideration for others. Thoughtless sex brought worries and trouble and disaster to many people.

When she'd discovered the difficulties created between her father and Maria Zakro, she had become even more emphatic in her mind about the need for the brain to control the body and the importance of restraint.

But she wanted him!

Slowly her hand tried to draw away from his, and he let it go—reluctantly, but he did let it go, nevertheless. Holding her hands tightly together in front of her, twisting them, as if the action would wring out her emotions and leave her dry, she stumbled up the beach to her towel and blindly and viciously rubbed her body with it.

For a little while, as her skin glowed with her administrations, he remained where she had left him, turning to stare at the sea, and then quietly returned with his head bent, not looking at her. Carefully she laid the towel on the sand and sat down to wait for him to dry himself. With a dazed expression, she faced the luminous, enamel water, its smoothness only broken at its edge where small waves curled like Ionic scrolls. Her hands, unable to be still, idly fingered the tiny woolly leaves of the sea medick beside her.

Although she could only see him out of the corner of her eye, Dimitri was filling her world. Every move he was making, each rasp of the towel over those black glossy hairs on his chest, each breath, every shift of his body, was magnified to such an intensity that it astonished her. Never had her senses been so finely tuned. He'd moved into her life more thoroughly than she had thought. Realisation wrenched at her heart. She loved him. She'd fallen head over heels for this dark, difficult man, whose compassion lay far beneath the surface and whose tough, lonely air made him impossible to be certain of. She could have fallen for an easier man. Someone who was hard up like her, and lived in a little terraced house. Not a man who walked daily in a palace! You fool, Helen, she told herself. You dreaming idiot.

Her body had stiffened with her discovery. Dimitri lay down beside her, drawing her inexorably with that irresistible quality of profound inner magnetism. Her back grew even more erect. They were supposed to be leaving; she ought to get up and remind him. Her limbs seemed heavy, her brain so muddled, and there was such a choking feeling in her throat that she was unable to move or speak.

'Helen, it's been a lovely day,' he said softly. 'I've enjoyed every minute, thanks to you. You're very easy to get along with. And did you find it hard, being in the presence of a rich man?'

She winced ruefully. 'No,' she said in a low tone. 'Sometimes . . . I forgot you were.'

'Good. There's hope for me yet.'

Helen didn't answer, but her ribcage rose with a sudden deep breath.

Dimitri groaned. 'Do me a favour, Helen, and don't breathe in. Just keep breathing out. Next time we go swimming, you might put on something a little less revealing, too. My heartbeat is giving me some problems, and I'm having difficulty keeping my eyes in their sockets.'

Despite herself, she had to laugh. 'This is the only

costume I have,' she said, looking down at her neat black bikini and the very feminine body within it. 'It was all I could . . .'

'I know. It was all you could push into your rucksack. What little corner did you find for it? Popped it into an eggcup, did you?'

He was relieving the tension and she was grateful. 'Idiot! It's not that small.'

'Nearly,' he said gloomily. 'Very nearly.'

The atmosphere tautened again. Helen stared stolidly out to sea, knowing that he was watching her all the time. Small curls of excitement began to thread through her body. Her jaw clenched with the pain of longing.

Without a word, Dimitri stood up and walked into the sea, swimming so far that the tormented Helen could hardly see his head bobbing in the water. The sky was beginning to turn a soft pink, and little purple clouds scudded over the sun. She shivered and dressed mechanically.

'I want to go back,' she said in a small voice when he approached, looking very serious.

'Yes. I'll just dry myself.'

They were both restrained. It seemed that they knew the danger of a look, a touch, a softness in the voice. Each recognised that the other was on the edge of control; neither dared to break that control. It had been such a short time since they'd met. They weren't really ready for the next stage. It *was* too soon. And yet . . . Helen knew that time would make no difference. Her feelings for Dimitri would never waver, even if he drew into his cold, loveless shell again. She'd glimpsed the man she loved, knew he was there, and would always yearn for him.

The silence that had fallen between them made Helen want to scream. He'd said they could go; she didn't want to be with him any longer, not like this, not wanting so badly and knowing her longing would be unfulfilled.

'I want to *go*,' she said in a small voice.

'In a minute.'

'Please!'

She felt Dimitri shift awkwardly beside her, and then knew he was checking his watch.

'It's getting late,' she complained. 'By the time we've driven all the way back . . .'

She broke off. He wasn't listening, only looking up at the helicopter that was flying off from deep in the gorge. She hadn't seen it return with Mrs Kastelli. In fact . . . it could have been at his house all day. Had he brought her here to get her out of the gorge so she didn't know that some important visitor was there? Oh, God! Helen's stomach plummeted. He couldn't have done that! This was a pleasant day out for both of them, wasn't it? There wasn't another reason that he'd taken her out, surely?

'Right, shall we go?' suggested Dimitri.

He began to pull on his shorts and Helen's shoulders slumped. He *had* been waiting for the helicopter to leave before taking her back. It was too much of a coincidence. It upset her even more that, now the coast was clear for them to return, he couldn't get back fast enough. Even when she watched the sponge fishermen sailing back into the bay with their catch, and asked if she could wait to watch them land, he had hurried her on.

The sunset was glorious, flooding the sky with scarlet and gold. It made her feel worse that they were in such wonderful surroundings and he was behaving deviously towards her. She sat in miserable silence for the whole journey back, and was almost relieved when they pulled up at her house.

Night had fallen, black velvet skies nurturing thousands of diamond stars and a huge moon. Helen pulled on a cardigan and gathered up her beachbag and wet towel.

'Thank you for coming with me today,' said Dimitri quietly. 'It's been one of the best days of my life.'

Her head lifted and slowly she turned to look at him with huge, unhappy eyes. He actually looked as if he meant that, she thought, wishing he did.

'Thank you,' she breathed, her throat constricting.

His hand reached out to cup the back of her head, but Helen forestalled him by shifting away, trembling from the hot arrows which had invaded her body at the thought of his kiss.

'Helen?' he queried softly. 'Don't be afraid of me. I'm not going to attack you. I was just hoping for a goodnight kiss, but I won't touch you if you'd prefer. To be honest, I think it would be better if you got out now.' He gave a brief laugh. 'The pleasure of the day, the memory of you in that bikini and the romance of this dark night are making me feel a little unsteady. Goodnight. Thanks again.'

'Goodnight,' she whispered, stumbling out.

'See you in the morning,' he called.

'What?'

'The orchid search,' he reminded her quietly. 'Wear your funny boots and I'll wear mine. That'll keep us sober.'

CHAPTER NINE

FAR into the night, Helen's candles burned. Try as she might, even with the help of two glasses of *raki,* she was unable to sleep. Instead, her thoughts went round and round on the same track: she loved a man who was so different from her that she marvelled they had any point of contact at all. It wouldn't work, the relationship was doomed. It was like Maria and her father; they had met, fused, exploded together and parted with tragic consequences.

So Helen prepared to list all of Dimitri's faults, but found herself dreamily thinking of the way his hair curled on the satin skin behind his ears, and the way his hand gave her such a sense of security that she never wanted to let go. It was hopeless, she thought crossly. He was in her system and determined to stay there!

She rose and paced the little bedroom in the brilliant light of the full moon. It was so bright that she could see right across the valley to Vronda. On an impulse, she hauled off her flimsy baby-doll nightie and dressed in a warm track-suit and trainers, not bothering to tie up her loose hair. Automatically she collected up her passport, without stopping to remove the documents inside it, and pushed it into her shoulder-bag. If she'd been thinking straight, she would have realised that burglars were unlikely to raid the little house. But her mind was on other things.

Outside was a warm, welcoming silence. She leaned against the trunk of an olive tree and attuned her ears to the peace that engulfed her. It was a false peace, of course, but it gave her brain a rest from the wild confusion for a while.

Her problems appeared unreal out here. In the magic of the valley, there was an illusion of timelessness and serenity that encouraged her to imagine she could let her heart take her where it wished and that everything would be all right.

That was silly, she scolded herself, pushing away from the tree and beginning to meander down the valley track. Far across the valley, a scops owl called, repeating its long, melancholy note at rhythmic intervals. The scent of herbs was overpowering. All day the sun had drawn out their oils, and as she brushed past the oregano, thyme and sage, great wafts of their heady spices drifted to her nostrils.

The Garden of Eden. And she had almost taken the apple and brought disaster on both their heads.

Helen walked on, letting the stillness of the night bring some kind of quiet to her soul, letting time stand still. She had reached the entrance to the gorge before she knew, and hesitated, wondering whether to return or not. Yet something drew her on. She wanted to look up at Dimitri's house and impress on herself that he was as inwardly distant, remote and unobtainable as that cold, friendless building. The sight of all that ostentatious wealth might bring her to her senses.

It seemed to take longer than she remembered in daylight, although she was glad when she finally saw it. King Minos's Palace! How stately it was, and what an air of hauteur it gave off! Helen forced herself to imagine meeting Dimitri's parents and walking around the palatial colonnades. She smiled ruefully at the incongruous sight of herself dressed as she was now in a chain-store track-suit, drinking coffee with an exquisitely gowned and coiffed Mrs Kastelli, and discussing the weather and the price of artichokes.

She was chuckling to herself, half-way between laughter and rueful regret, when she became aware of a rustling in the undergrowth. Her mind scanned the possibilities, knowing that quite small animals could make what seemed to be a lot of noise at night.

A polecat? Badger? Fox? Nothing that would harm her,
anyway. Still, she felt nervous. She'd go back now.

There was a low growl and she froze, feeling the hairs of
her body standing on end. Slowly she turned her head to see
a huge mastiff, barring her way out! Oh, God! she
thought. It must be one of Dimitri's hounds!

'*Ella, Ella,*' she whispered, remembering that Cretan dogs
sounded fierce but could be pacified if you called them in a
friendly tone. This one didn't seem to know that fact. It
bared its teeth in a terrifying snarl. '*Ella, Ella,*' she said,
trying to disguise her fear.

The dog's hackles were raised, its head lowered. It took one
menacing step forwards, and Helen's panic overwhelmed her
common sense; she ran like a hare, deeper into the gorge, not
knowing where she went or why, only that the dog was close
behind. It would have to catch up with her soon! What would
she do? She sobbed, her breath catching in her lungs. Stones
fell on to the path beside her as she ran, and she looked up in
alarm. A black figure had appeared, right on the top of the
cliff, a figure that was shouting something.

Helen threw a terrified glance over her shoulder, to see
that the dog had stopped and was watching the man above
for instructions.

'Please don't let him hurt me!' she screamed. 'I'm
harmless! I just wanted a walk! Please keep him off!'

Then she realised. In her demented state, she hadn't
recognised that the voice had been Dimitri's. She was safe!
Weeping with relief, she sank to the ground as her legs gave
way. The dog twitched as she did so, but he stayed where his
master had told him.

Feeling sick, she tucked her head between her knees, only
dimly aware that Dimitri was climbing down the steep cliff
towards her. She heard his feet land with a thud, and then he
rapped out another command to the dog. Her neck prickled

at the sound of its panting very close to her. As she slowly raised her head, she saw that the huge dog stood in front of her and was fixing her with its malicious eyes. Helen swallowed, hardly daring to let even her lashes flicker.

'What are you up to?'

Her eyes widened at the glacial tones. Keeping a wary check on the dog, she flicked a glance at Dimitri. He looked sinister and menacing in black leather, his dark face hard and uncompromising.

'Dimitri, I was only walking,' she said shakily.

'At night?' he scorned.

'Yes!'

'Why?'

'I couldn't sleep,' she said defiantly. 'Call your dog off. I'm not likely to hurt you.'

'He's trained to guard intruders like that.'

There was no softness in his voice at all, no sign that they'd even met before. Helen despaired. 'I'm not an intruder,' she said miserably. 'I'm Helen and you know me. We had a lovely day on the beach, remember?' she added with bitterness.

'You're trespassing. You are acting suspiciously. I would be failing in my duty if I didn't question you about your odd behaviour.'

'Duty? Damn your duty!' she cried, her voice shaking with suppressed anger. The dog was too close for her to do what she wanted: jump up and pummel Dimitri's arrogant body until he gasped!

'You may have no sense of responsibility, but I have,' he said coldly. 'You disappoint me, Helen. I have trusted you with a great deal of information, and now I am forced to wonder whether that trust was misplaced. I want to know what you're doing here. Somehow I don't think I have the whole story.'

'I'm sorry if I ran off the track,' she said defiantly. 'But so

would you, if you were being chased by a massive great dog
with vicious teeth and a heart-stopping snarl!'

'You said you couldn't sleep?' he asked grimly, not
smiling at her description at all.

'I—oh, Dimitri, you know what happened on the island! I
had to think.' She took a closer look at him and saw that his
face was dark with stubble and his eyes hollow. 'You're
awake too, and it's the middle of the night. Perhaps you had
to do some thinking.'

'You're damn right, I did!' he rasped. 'I had to work out
what had hit me! I had to think why you didn't let me make
love to you, why you pushed me away.'

'And?' she prompted, knowing it was pointless
pretending she hadn't longed for him.

He snapped at the dog, who backed off. Then Dimitri
crouched down in front of Helen and held her with his
glittering eyes.

'You were struggling with yourself. You wanted me as
much as I wanted you, and yet you couldn't allow yourself to
surrender. I think that's because you were dismayed that
your emotions were mixing with business—you *are* here for a
specific purpose, and the only thing I can think of is that it's
something to do with slipping through my security net.'

'That's not true!' she flashed.

'Really?' His eyebrow rose coolly. 'You arrive here,
appearing to be on holiday, knowing exactly where Maria's
house is, as if you'd been carefully briefed. You fight all
opposition that I put up to your presence, even to the extent
of refusing free accommodation elsewhere—at one stage in
the most exclusive hotel in Greece. I find you taking photographs with a high-powered camera, and you examine my
house with binoculars which are even more powerful. You
take notes and draw maps in a notebook . . .' Helen's eyes
squeezed shut at the cold, relentless voice. He was mercilessly listing his suspicions and that tore at her heart.

'. . . you switch from being antagonistic to being encouraging to me. You ask to be taken to the Cretan Palace. When I question you, I hear some story about Flower Walks. Flower Walks! Do you think I was born yesterday? I've dealt with terrorists. I've foiled would-be assassins and abductors. You wouldn't believe the stories they used for cover—nearly as unbelievable as yours!'

Helen's eyes shot open and she flushed at his scorn. 'Investigate!' she spat. 'Go on, investigate me! You'll find that I am a researcher for John Fraser.'

'I've done that,' he said grimly. 'Your cover is good. You even know something about flowers. That doesn't stop you being used by some man you're living with.'

'I'm not!' she cried, incensed, her blonde hair swinging wildly as she shook her head.

'Hard to believe,' he sneered. 'You're too sensual and have an instinct for sex. And you're easily aroused.'

'You swine!' If the dog hadn't been watching her every move hungrily, she would have hit him for that insult. As it was, she had to content herself with clenching and unclenching her fists.

'Anyway, you have a problem. John Fraser denies that you are working on a project. He says you are on holiday.'

Of course, he'd be careful divulging her business to a stranger, she thought! John knew her presence in Crete was a delicate situation.

'That's because of competition! He'd never let on to anyone what his next plans were,' she cried, furious that Dimitri had trusted her so little that he'd looked into her background. All the time they'd been on the island, he'd . . . 'When did you find this out?' she asked in icy tones.

'When I got back last night,' he answered painfully. 'And now, I find you lurking about beneath my house. So explain—and don't make up stories about botanists eagerly trotting along the rights of way. I'm not buying that one.'

'It's all true, and they *are* my rights of way. I——'

Helen was stopped in mid-sentence when Dimitri grabbed her shoulders, his grip like steel.

'*My* rights of way?' he grated, his face a few inches from hers. 'Did you say *my*? Are you telling me that you've bought the house and its land from Maria?'

'You're hurting,' she breathed.

His face and his hands were unyielding. 'Answer me.'

'The house and land and rights of way are mine, yes,' she whispered.

He was very still, his eyes searching hers. 'Now tell me where she is,' he said in a terrible, agonised voice.

'Why? Why do you want to know? What is it about Maria Zakro that makes you and that guard of yours on the road so nervous?' she asked.

'I have to trace her,' he said. 'It's vital. I want to make sure she keeps away from here. I'll pay her well to do so.'

Helen's face filled with bitter mockery. At least she could take pleasure in thwarting him.

'You'll have a job,' she said harshly. 'Maria's dead.'

'*What?*' Dimitri's hands dropped lifelessly from her shoulders. 'When?' he demanded.

'Over twenty years ago,' she said, some inner caution telling her not to be accurate. He was too perceptive: he might put two and two together and realise she was Maria's child. Stubbornly, Helen wanted Dimitri to trust her because of some inner feeling, not because she explained everything to him. Then her attention was taken by the look on Dimitri's face. It had drawn into lines of shock, his eyes staring emptily, the mouth a thin, downward curve. By the light of the deceptive moon, it appeared that his tanned skin had become ashen.

'Twenty years. Twenty years,' he repeated in a whisper. 'My *God*!' Helen jumped at his yell. 'All those years of hate and fear . . .' He made an effort to control his simmering

fury. 'Who did you buy the house from, then?' he shot out.
'Her heir? Tell me, Helen, you must tell me!'

'Stop shouting at me!' she yelled. 'I won't tell you! I
won't be bullied by you! I'm sorry I trespassed, and you
know why. Everything I've told you about myself is true. I
was walking because I couldn't sleep and wanted to calm my
mind. I didn't expect to be chased by vicious dogs and be
subjected to accusations!' She tried to rise but was held
down. 'Let me get up! I want to go home!'

'You'll tell me,' he seethed, 'if I have to force you to.'

'No! I won't!' Helen was blinded with hot, angry tears, but
this time Dimitri didn't offer tender sympathy.

'In that case,' he said harshly, 'I'm going to have to work
on you until you will. Get up!'

'What . . .' She was roughly dragged to her feet and
quivered with indignation. Dimitri pushed his hands under
her armpits and marched her along the path. 'What are you
doing?' she yelled. 'How dare you manhandle me like this!'

'Shut up and come quietly. It'll hurt less,' he snarled.
'The more you struggle, the tighter I hold you, and the more
bruises you end up with.'

'You cruel, vicious . . .'

'Enough!' he roared. Was it her imagination, or did that
word break at the end as if he, too, was in despair? Helen's
tears flowed in bewildered distress and angry frustration.
'I'm taking you up the mountain,' he said, breathing
heavily in an obvious effort to keep his temper and speak
clearly. 'You can go up it the easy way, on your own two
feet, or I can drag you. Make up your mind quickly, and be
absolutely certain that I intend to get you there one way or
another.'

'I'll scream——'

'No one will hear you except the guards at the house, and
they know I'm searching for you. They'll realise that I've
found you and am dealing with you as I choose.'

'Oh, my God!' whispered Helen.

'Walk or be dragged?'

'Walk, you callous swine,' she said through her teeth.

She felt nothing inside her now, only a black emptiness. Dimitri's true colours were showing, and she despised him for what he was: a merciless man without a heart who would stop at nothing to get whatever he wanted. Where was the man she loved?

It was a long, long climb up the snaking path. She felt cold as the mountain air began to bite, and Dimitri silently shrugged off his jacket when he noticed her shivering. At first she refused it, but his mouth compressed in an angry line and he continued to hold the jacket out. Listlessly she pulled its soft folds around her, feeling near to crying again when she found it was still warm from his body and smelt of him, too.

The moon was occasionally hidden by a cloud, and Dimitri would then reach out to hold her elbow and guide her so that she didn't scratch herself on the low mounds of thorny burnet. Then they came to a plateau, and Helen saw to her surprise that it held the ruins of an ancient settlement.

'Lissos,' said Dimitri curtly, watching her eyes travel over the huge Inca-style wall of massive, unmortared blocks of stone. 'Don't try running anywhere. There are sheer drops on either side.'

They walked over a path of silver stones eaten with age. It must have been an impregnable site. The main buildings could only be reached by a narrow ridge about a hundred yards long and about four yards wide. Helen could see an awesome blackness each side of the unprotected path, and Dimitri held out his hand to her before they crossed.

She tossed her head, her long golden hair swirling angrily, and she took a step forwards. But he had grabbed her and held her close to his body, one arm around her waist like an iron band.

'Damn you, Helen' he muttered. 'Don't be so stubborn. Sometimes strong winds can gust up here. I don't want you blown over the precipice.'

'No,' she said scathingly. 'Not till you have all the information you want.'

The muscles in his body clenched. Helen felt the heat of him as they slowly traversed the ridge, and groaned inwardly when she realised that he still had the power to arouse her. When they reached the other side, he released her as if she was something unpleasant.

'In there,' he growled.

Her heavy head lifted to look up at the mountain refuge hut—or perhaps it was a shepherd's hut, she wasn't sure. It could even have been used by the Zakro family, when they had grazed their flocks. Set among the archaic ruins of the long-forgotten hill town, it must have an incomparable view in daylight. At night, though, and under these circumstances, Helen thought it looked sinister.

'What are you going to do?' she whispered, resisting the pressure of his hand as he guided her up an ancient stone stairway.

'Anything I have to, to get the truth from you,' he said answered coldly.

Helen knew that, once they were inside the hut, her chances of escape were virtually nil. She had to make her bid now.

'Oh, Dimitri!' she faltered, pretending to buckle at the knees.

'Helen! Sweetheart!'

She'd turned like lightning and had begun to race back over the high causeway, her heart thumping, her brain registering suddenly that his voice had sounded terribly concerned and contrite! The discovery made her stumble over one of the rough stones and she fell headlong, just as Dimitri caught up with her. It was his arms which saved her from smashing her face on to the stones, or breaking an arm, because he threw himself valiantly forwards to land on his back beneath her, and she thudded hard on to his body.

For several seconds Helen couldn't move, since the fall had winded her. His body was softer than the ground, of course, but it was still hard and unyielding. She shifted slightly and immediately groaned.

Dimitri's arms held her tightly and his hands soothed.

'You're hurt,' he murmured. 'You shouldn't have run like that.'

'I wanted to get away from you!' she wailed in a wobbly voice, biting down the pain that jack-knifed up her leg from her left ankle.

His body stiffened and the wonderful comfort of his arms was removed as he dropped them to his sides.

'See if you can get up,' he said woodenly. 'I can't lie here all night.'

Awkwardly, she rolled over and sat up, nursing her ankle. It throbbed and felt swollen. Dimitri struggled to a sitting position.

'Are you hurt, too?' she asked, alert to his grey, strained face.

'I'll live,' he said curtly. 'What's the matter with your foot?'

With trembling fingers, Helen tried to undo her shoelace.

'Let me.' Dimitri grimly pushed away her hands and loosened the laces thoroughly before gingerly beginning to remove the training shoe. His dark eyes constantly flickered to Helen's face, gauging the amount of pain he was inflicting. 'I'm sorry, but I have to do this,' he said tightly. 'Hang on to me and dig your nails in when it hurts.'

She stretched out a hesitant hand and gripped his shoulder as hard as she could. He was only wearing a thin shirt because she had his jacket, and she felt how cold he was. She winced. He was being as gentle as possible, but the heavy throbbing made her feel sick. Overcome with nausea, she bent her head forward and leaned against his shoulder. A sympathetic arm came around her back and stroked it for a few moments.

Helen felt like weeping. She almost wished he wouldn't act in a humane way, that he would remain cold and hard. Having his tender care directed towards her was too much to bear.

'Don't do that,' she complained.

'My apologies,' he said stiffly. 'It's my automatic response to females in distress.'

She noticed he didn't use the word 'ladies', and felt riled by his slight.

'I don't like you touching me,' she said haughtily.

'You'll have to put up with it for a while till I have your shoe off,' he snapped. 'It won't be long.'

His last words sounded sympathetic again, and she noticed he was worrying over the way her face scrunched up in pain.

'You don't have to be nice to me,' she said. 'I'm surprised you don't yank the shoe off and be done with it.'

'Don't tempt me,' he growled. 'You've been nothing but trouble ever since you arrived. I must have been mad not to let you jump off the precipice.'

'I wasn't intending to do that,' she cried. 'I'm not *that* afraid of you.'

Dimitri's mouth wrenched into a savage snarl. With slow, deliberate care, he laid her foot on his knee and then felt in his pocket, bringing out a wicked-looking knife.

'Dimitri!' she gasped, her hands clapped to her mouth.

'Relax,' he growled. 'I'm only going to cut your foot off.'

'Ha ha,' she said coldly as he sliced off her sock.

The cool mountain air gave some relief to the throbbing flesh. Dimitri prodded and probed and turned her foot about, then proclaimed that it wasn't broken, only sprained.

'We'd better get you into the warm,' he said, glancing at the hut.

'That's warm?' she said in a disbelieving voice.

'It will be soon.' Gasping a little and moving stiffly, he got to his feet, bent and picked Helen up. 'Good thing you're only a pocket Venus,' he muttered.

Helen said nothing. To keep her balance, she had to place her arms around his neck, and it was a terrifyingly pleasurable sensation, being carried by him and feeling the smoothness of his neck, the gloss of his hair and the warmth of his skin under her fingers. Utterly weary, and knowing she was well and truly in his power, she dropped her head against his chest and he snuggled her into him more securely.

This could have been very romantic, she thought gloomily. His ribcage became warm against her body and was sweet torment to her soul. He was so big and strong and handsome; so much the man she had seen in her dreams. He was the kind of man you could rely on in an emergency, who would take over and handle any situation with a calm flair. Her heart thudded loudly. She placed one hand on his chest to keep herself a little away from him, so he didn't notice her reaction. And realised that his heart was thudding violently under her palm.

The bright moonlight lit the inside of the house with silver. It was similar to her place, though when Dimitri had placed her on a soft, convertible sofa-bed and elevated her foot, he went around lighting the candles and she saw that the hut was furnished in a contemporary style.

With evident skill, Dimitri lit the stove. So much for not knowing about them, she thought, sending him a ferocious glare. He ignored it and settled down to bathing her foot in flesh-numbing water.

'Keep still,' he frowned when she tried to draw away. 'It'll bring down the swelling. I imagine you don't want to be here for weeks.'

'Weeks? But . . . Can't you get your helicopter to take me off?'

'It's nowhere near here.'

'You mean I'm stuck in this place?' she cried in horror.

'Correct. For a little while, at least, until you feel the ankle can take your weight with a little support from me. However, it will be a good opportunity for you to tell me about yourself,' he said smugly.

'That's the last thing I'll do!'

'Then be prepared for a long stay. There's enough food here to keep a party of climbers or four hungry shepherds for months. The menu could get a trifle repetitious, but it'll be nourishing.'

'You wouldn't dare,' she challenged. He was bluffing, she knew he must be.

There was a gleam in his eyes and a sensual curve to his mouth as he answered, 'I dare. Don't underestimate me, Helen. I play to win. And I think you'll admit defeat within twenty-four hours and surrender to me.'

'Su-su-surrender?' she squeaked. 'You mean you're staying here, too?'

'Of course,' he said smoothly, sitting down on the sofa beside her, his arms on either side. Helen pressed herself back in fear as his dark, determined face hovered a few inches from hers. 'There are one or two things I want from you, Helen, and I fully intend to get them!'

CHAPTER TEN

GRUDGINGLY, Helen had to admit that Dimitri made her as comfortable as possible. He'd found a first-aid box and strapped her ankle expertly, then collected bedding from a huge wooden chest and temporarily tucked her up in an armchair while he made up the bed-settee. She'd opted to have a snack and a warm drink in the chair rather than in bed, and he left her there to busy himself with opening tins. For the first time, he turned his back to her and she was horrified to see that there was blood on his shirt.

Her involuntary gasp made him whirl around.

'What is it?' he demanded irritably when he saw she was still safely in the same position, with her foot up on a stool. 'I nearly cut myself.'

'You're bleeding!' she cried. 'On your back. You'd better let me look.'

His hand reached around to feel, and he glanced at the slight smear on his fingers. 'Nothing much. Only a graze.'

'Oh, very macho,' she said witheringly. 'Afraid of a little nursing?'

His eyes brooded and Helen quivered at the intensity of their depths.

'As a matter of fact, yes,' he answered quietly, returning to the stove.

She tried to make out what he meant. She was hardly likely to injure him while his back was turned to her; she depended on him, after all. That could only mean . . . He was afraid of his lust for her. It would get in the way of his determination to interrogate her thoroughly. No, that

136

couldn't be right: if he wanted, he could take everything.

'Here,' he said abruptly, handing out a steaming dish of tinned *moussaka*.

'Aren't you having any?' she asked, noticing that he had made himself a dish of tinned vegetables.

'It's Lent. I don't eat meat or fish.'

'Are you telling me that you were even lying to me when we first met?' she asked in astonishment. 'That you reeled off that mouth-watering menu just to make me feel worse?'

Dimitri bit his lip. 'You know I was trying to make you want to go home at that stage. I found the menu just as tempting. I miss eating meat. It's quite a sacrifice for me.'

'No wonder you're so bad-tempered,' she said sharply.

'Eat.'

For a moment, Helen bristled at his tone and fully intended to start an argument, but the aroma of the food was drifting to her nostrils and she discovered she was starving. Her anger with him and any understanding of his behaviour would wait! She ate every last morsel, taking a kind of pleasure in the fact that Dimitri eyed her meal with sullen envy. Warmer and less hungry, she downed two cups of hot chocolate made from dried chocolate and milk powders, thinking that it seemed an odd set-up for shepherds: first aid kits and tinned stores.

'Who uses this place?' she asked curiously.

He chewed his lip, considering whether to answer her or not. 'Four men from Vronda run sheep and goats up here in the high summer,' he said. 'I keep the hut provisioned in case there's a storm or one of them has to stay up here. I also use the hut. I come up here for days at a time.'

'I see.' Helen thought how lonely he must be. 'If you let them come up here, why can't my walkers? They'd be under supervision.'

'Because of security. I keep telling you. My father has known the men all his life and trusts them. They're honest men who have no desire for wealth and therefore cannot be bribed by potential trouble-makers. They don't realise the extent of my father's business, anyway.'

'It's very remote. Is there a telephone?' she asked hopefully, trying to remember whether there had been any wires to the house. 'We could ask for help and you could tell your parents where you are. They'll be worried if you don't turn up for breakfast.'

He looked amused. 'No telephone. It wouldn't be much of a retreat for me if there was. And my parents never have any idea whether I'll be at home or not. I come and go as I please without consulting them. I'm often out for breakfast.'

'Oh.'

Not so lonely, then, thought Helen. Sometimes he spent his mornings lying in bed with women. Sharp, souring jealousy ripped through her and she was ashamed . He'd seen the pain in her eyes and she dropped her lashes to conceal the overwhelming sense of hopelessness.

'Your ankle must hurt badly,' he said softly. 'I am sorry. I can give you something for the pain if you like.'

Her velvet brown eyes widened. A kiss. That was the only thing which would make her forget all her pain.

'Like . . . what?' she asked, unable to keep her voice steady.

'Damn you!' he raged, leaping to his feet and striding around the room. 'Don't *lure* me in that way! I will not be seduced by you!'

'Oh! I've never known such an arrogant man!' she seethed, furious with her own transparency and the fact that he had rejected her. 'Just because every woman you've ever met has fallen at your feet doesn't mean I want to! You're reading the signals wrongly!'

'No, I'm not,' he muttered, pausing and gripping the back of the sofa, his eyes a glittering jet. 'I know women too well. I've had half a lifetime of being lured. If you've finished eating, I'll help you into bed.'

'Vain man!' Helen thought for a moment. 'I want to use the bathroom first,' she said, embarrassed.

Dimitri nodded and helped her up, his strong arm locking under her armpit and around her body. With his help, she hopped over to the back room and shut the door firmly on him. She managed to freshen herself up, suddenly feeling very tired indeed. Seeing this when she emerged, he carried her back to the couch and laid her down gently, as if she was a piece of porcelain china.

'What are you doing?' she protested, as he began to unzip the jacket.

'You're not sleeping in that. It's getting very warm in here and I'll keep the stove going all night. The air temperature outside will probably go below zero in an hour or so. I suggest we take off that track-suit top and bottom, too.'

'We?'

He shrugged. 'All right, you.'

Settling himself down next to her on the low, wide bed, he folded his arms and waited.

'I don't think I will,' she said nervously.

'You'll be very hot.'

'Then I'll have to be hot, won't I?' she muttered, frowning as he thoughtfully removed her other shoe and sock and tucked her in.

'Sleep well,' he mocked.

The candles were doused and Helen lay for a while in the flickering firelight, listening to Dimitri trying to make himself comfortable in the armchair. She hoped he would have a bad night. Gradually the tide of sleep crept over her.

In the early hours she woke, tossing off the quilted duvet in the stuffy heat. By the glow of the stove, she could see that Dimitri's eyes were shut; he was fast asleep. Surreptitiously, she slid off her top, glad that she wore a vest-style T-shirt underneath, even if it was rather revealing. She looked down at the trousers doubtfuly. They were baggy, so she should be able to wriggle them over her injured foot. Sitting up, she slid them from off her hips and freed her right foot. So far, so good. But when it came to raising her left foot, she found that it hurt too much, and stared down at it in frustration, wondering what to do.

'Stubborn woman,' growled a voice in her ear.

She shot into the air and yelled at the pain from her ankle, finding herself clasped in Dimitri's arms and held tightly against his naked chest.

'You beast! You did that on purpose!' she grated into what seemed an acre of warm, muscled flesh.

'Don't be ridiculous!'

He drew away and Helen could see that he was very angry. Ignoring her protests, he removed the track-suit trousers and placed them carefully on a chair. Automatically, her knee came to angle across her small lacy briefs. She felt dreadfully exposed. Her hands fluttered first at her breasts and then on her thighs.

Dimitri faced her and Helen found herself trembling at the sight of him. In the intimate surroundings, with the flickering red light playing on his naked torso, he looked magnificent and infinitely desirable. His eyes watched her, swept to her parted lips and to her quickly rising breasts under the thin top.

He took a deep breath. 'You are the most sensual woman I have ever known in the whole of my life,' he said huskily.

Helen's tongue slicked over dry lips.

'Very effective,' he drawled. 'Any more tricks?'

'Go back to sleep,' she croaked.

'I don't imagine I could for one minute,' he said softly. 'I'm a little too red-blooded for this situation.'

With a meaningful look in his eyes, he strode towards her.

'No,' she cried, trying in vain to move away before he reached the bed.

'You are trapped by your own actions,' he said silkily, placing his hands on her shoulders and pushing her back on to the mattress. 'And I think it's time for a little action on my part.'

'No!' Her head twisted away desperately, but Dimitri calmly caught her chin between thumb and forefinger and turned it back, angling it ready for his kiss.

Helen watched in fascinated suspense as his head lowered—slowly, very slowly, far too slowly. The sultriness of his dark, passionate face made her explode inside. With a moan of intense need, she reached out her arms and pulled his head hard down so that their mouths met in a savage kiss. The ferocity of her own feelings frightened her, but she couldn't stop. He was lying beside her now, murmuring passionately in Greek, lost in the same world of heated desire as she, and they plundered and devoured each other's mouths with a hunger born of unfulfilled arousal.

Dimly, Helen was aware that he was careful of her injured foot, and that his back *was* grazed—quite badly. Her fingers slowed in their frantic caresses of his spine and explored gently.

'No,' he said harshly. 'Forget that. Think only of this.'

His mouth ground into hers again and then was touring her throat, sending flames of heat into Helen's loins with the sensuality of his kisses and the demand of his hands. This was no gentle, cautious loving. They both had reached a point where only a frenzy of passion could release them.

Dimitri's relentless hands pushed up her T-shirt and then he was growling his approval in his throat as he took each breast in his mouth in turn, bringing them to their ultimate fullness, teasing each peak to a throbbing, rosy nub that he suckled with electrifying result.

A deep shudder ran through Helen. 'Oh, Dimitri!' she whispered, hardly aware of what she was saying or how much her tone betrayed her need.

Hastily he pulled off her top and stared at her, his eyes dark and inscrutable. Then his mouth swooped again, to her eyes, whispering over her ears, her lips, the hollow of her throat, and she felt his hands beginning to remove her briefs. Her thighs squeezed together tightly.

Dimitri merely slid down her body and kissed her waist, bemusing her again, and she found herself gripping a fistful of his hair in sweet agony as his fingers gently slid between her thighs and moved rhythmically over the delicate lace that barred his way.

'*Ohhh!*' she groaned deeply with an outrush of breath. 'Please, Dimitri, please stop! I can't bear it any longer!'

'Neither can I,' he whispered, moving up her body again, his teeth nibbling flesh as he did. 'Lift your body a little.'

His hand had grasped her briefs as if to draw them down. 'No, you don't understand,' she said, her voice cracking from lack of air. It seemed that every part of her was concentrated on the points of the body he was touching, rubbing, caressing . . . 'Ohh!' she moaned. 'Leave me alone, I don't want to go any further. I don't know how I let you go this far! I'm confused! You've used your clever wiles on me, Dimitri Kastelli, and taken advantage of me!'

'You don't mean that, Helen,' he said, still moving his fingers with that indescribable delicacy of touch. 'We want each other. Why shouldn't we make love? I'll be very careful not to hurt your foot.'

'My foot? Dear God, I——' She hesitated and then decided to risk his laughter and sarcasm. 'Dimitri, you can't make love to me. I'm not going to let any man make love to me until I'm married. In fact, you've . . . you've gone further than anyone, ever.'

He grew very still. With evident reluctance, he drew his fingers away and carefully lifted himself over to one side, where he lay, face-down, with his head driven into the pillow, his fists tightly clenched and his whole body tensed like a bow-string. Eventually his legs slid to the floor and he went over to pour himself a drink of *raki*.

'Want some?' he said in an expressionless voice, pouring himself a second tumblerful.

'Water, please,' she said in relief. He had some principles, it seemed. She sipped the icy water and looked at him from under her lashes. He appeared to be finding it difficult to know what do with himself, taking a few feral strides, stopping, turning, striding again . . .

'I don't know whether to believe you or not,' he growled.

'I'm not going to let you find out,' she said quickly. 'But it's true. You can laugh if you like, but I'm a virgin and I intend to stay one until my wedding night.'

'Laugh?' He didn't look in the least as if he wanted to do so. 'The laugh is on me, Helen.' He ran a hand through his hair. 'I'm not sure I can stay in this room with you.'

'Then find a way to get me off this moutain!' she cried in desperation.

'I can't do that,' he said harshly. 'Not until you tell me why you're here and who you bought the Zakro property from—and their whereabouts.'

Helen closed her eyes and groaned. He was relentless. There was no point in holding out any longer. No purpose was to be served in taking pleasure at the frustration of his demands—as far as information was concerned, that was!

'First you must tell me honestly why you are so anxious to know,' she said in a defeated tone.

'All right.' He came close to her, holding out his hands in a placatory manner when she shrank back. 'I'm only intending to sit down,' he said quickly, the bed depressing as he did so.

'You won't touch me?'

His mouth twisted. 'Despoil a virgin? I have no wish to be the first man in a woman's life. Virgins are notoriously emotional about sex. You are enough of a thorn in my side, without becoming dependent on me.'

'You——'

'Let's get on with this,' he said irritably. 'It'll be dawn soon. We both lay our cards on the table and I get you off the mountain somehow. Agreed?'

'Agreed,' she said miserably, wondering what would happen to her then.

'I understand that Maria had a child. I have to trace that child. He or she could ruin me. It's not possible for me to explain why, because others are involved, but if I fail to find him—or her—then everything that my father has sacrificed his life for could be destroyed, and thousands of people could be out of a job. I can't stand idly by and see the business wantonly smashed: that would make his whole existence almost meaningless, and mine, since my life has been to serve the Kastelli empire. Then there are the dependent relatives of all of us, and it's due to that Jezebel called Maria Zakro, and her bastard!'

'Don't you *dare* call my moth . . .' Helen's furious voice trailed away as her throat constricted in fear at the sight of Dimitri's eyes, blazing with a terrible light.

'*What* did you say?' His words were barely audible.

Helen shut her eyes then found herself being violently shaken. Terrified, she looked up to see that Dimitri was almost beside himself with fury . . . and some other terrible emotion that she couldn't identify.

'Maria Zakro is my mother,' she said nervously. 'That's why I have her house and all her papers. That's why I'm here, to . . .'

'No! It isn't true, Helen, say you're lying! God in heaven, you *must* be lying!' he raged. 'Whatever you think of me, whatever tricks or jokes or revenge you're planning, don't lie about this! Tell me that it isn't true!'

'I can't do that! Sometimes I wish I could! Look at my passport in the front pocket of my bag—my birth certificate and all the papers relating to my house are in there! I brought them to Crete in case there was trouble when I took over the house. I can prove it to you! She *was* my mother!'

'Dear God! How old are you?' he whispered, reaching for her bag and slowly taking the papers out.

'Twenty-five.'

He hid his face in his hands. 'And I wanted . . . May the gods save me!'

'I don't understand,' she said, shocked at the intense horror in his voice. 'What did she do? Why are you so upset?'

'I can't explain,' he said shakily. 'I—oh, God! I don't know what . . . . Tell me about it, whatever you know,' he said, his haunted eyes making her heart ache.

'Well, she left Vronda to work in Agios Nikolaos and met my father in a taverna,' she began in a tremulous voice.

'Your father?' he said, puzzled.

'Yes, Dad. Dick Summers.'

'Your father is Dick Summers?' he repeated stupidly.

'Yes, I keep telling you. He—he—well, they made love and then she was pregnant, and then she came to England and I was born and then she died,' Helen babbled incoherently.

'Summers is the name on your birth certificate?' He checked, and some of the furrows on his brows were ironed out. 'Mother . . . Maria Zakro,' he muttered, reading aloud. 'God!'

'Dimitri, what . . .'

'You didn't know of this?' he asked, a ferocious scowl on his face.

'No!' she answered quickly, frightened at the change in him. There was a terrible pain in his eyes, a deep anguish and . . . almost horror. What was so awful about her being Maria's daughter? Why . . .

'You never looked at your birth certificate?' he probed.

'No, I didn't. Why should I? Dad kept it with all important papers in his strong-box. The first time I needed it was when I landed my first job abroad for the travel agency I work for. Because I was terribly overworked, clearing up everything outstanding on my desk before I left, Dad handled the form-filling and so on. It was only when Liz died that Dad told me. Can you imagine the shock?'

'Shock?' he laughed unpleasantly. 'I wish to God I could exchange your shock for mine,' he muttered.

Disappointed at his lack of sympathy, Helen missed the full meaning of his words. 'That's not very kind! It isn't easy discovering the mother you loved had no blood tie with you, and your real mother is a stranger from another country!'

'No. Of course. I'm sorry.' He passed a tired hand over his face, and Helen flinched at the deeply etched lines she saw there.

They both jumped at a brilliant flash of light which lit up the whole room. Dimitri strode over to the window and stood there for several moments, his shoulders slumped.

'What's the matter?' asked Helen.

A low rumble of thunder filled the air, and she could hear rain falling in torrents. 'That's the matter,' he said, his lips white. 'A storm. We may not be able to leave the mountain this morning, after all.'

Helen's body sagged. She couldn't stand much more of this atmosphere.

'We had a bargain,' she said. 'You promised to tell me your side of the situation.' She *had* to know why he was so upset.

'Yes.' He stretched and winced.

'You *are* hurt. Turn around,' she said, all thoughts of interrogating him forgotten in her loving concern. In his tired and defeated state, Dimitri seemed compliant and did as she asked. 'You're a mass of bruises! Get the first-aid box and I'll put something on them or you'll be terribly stiff.

And you really ought to have those deep grazes cleaned.'

He sighed deeply but did so, squatting down on the floor with his back to her so that she could roll over and reach him more easily. Gently she applied ointment to the bruised muscle and bone, lingering longer than necessary as she smoothed it in.

'Is that all right?' she asked softly. 'I'm not hurting you, am I?'

'No,' he snapped ungraciously. 'Get on with it.'

'You are a sour, bad-tempered man,' she observed crisply.

Sharp edges of stone had dug into his back and she wiped around the gashes tenderly. He had a lovely back, she mused, broad strong shoulders, a straight spine and a tapering waist. All with satin-smooth skin which felt sensational to touch. Her fingers slowed, massaging lightly, using the excuse to touch him for what was probably the last time. His body relaxed and his head rolled back.

'God, I'm exhausted,' he breathed.

'Then relax. Does that feel good?' she asked shakily.

'Mmmm.' He was almost asleep. Helen realised he probably hadn't done more than close his eyes in the armchair. It wasn't built for a big man to sleep in.

He gave a deep sigh. 'It feels . . . *God, Helen!*' he yelled, making her jump at the volume of sound in the small room. He had leapt up and was backing away. *'Hell!* We *have* to get out of here!'

As if to mock him, lightning tore into the room and he thumped the wall in frustrated fury.

'Will you let me know what's the matter?' she cried. 'Let me help you! It has something to do with my mother, hasn't it? You talked of being destroyed. How would she destroy you?'

'She already has,' he breathed, his eyes shut tightly.

Helen froze when he opened them again. He was in

torment!

'*Dimitri!* For God's sake, what is it?' she croaked.

And then he looked at her in a way she was never to forget for the whole of her life.

'I am your brother.'

CHAPTER ELEVEN

A LONG, terrible silence filled the air, suffocating them. This was the worst moment in Helen's life. Her mind was trying to take in what he had said, trying to make sense of all the contradictory messages filling her head.

Her brother?

Impossible. Inconceivable. For some reason he was convinced of the truth of his words. But . . . In an attempt to clear her head, she shook it.

'I don't understand: you've got different parents to me,' she began, voicing her thoughts. As she spoke, she tried to blot out the way he looked, the despair and misery on his face. For that made his claim even more possible, and she wouldn't accept that. She couldn't believe that they had very nearly made love and that she loved him more than anyone she had ever known. A man and woman kind of love, not that between sister and brother. There was nothing sisterly about the way she thought of Dimitri, not even as he sat in that terrible hunched-up way, looking as though the world had stopped spinning for him and would never start again. Helen wanted to take him in her arms, tell him his worries were all madness and let him kiss her till he had forgotten his stupid words. 'We don't even look alike,' she said in desperation. He seemed so certain.

'You'd better listen to me,' he said wearily. 'I thought the situation was bad enough without this! Wait a minute, I'll make some coffee. I can hardly keep awake.'

There was that awful silence again, a silence that transcended the slight sound of Dimitri boiling the water

149

and putting coffee into mugs, or the relentless rain
drumming on the roof and the ancient stones outside. It
could be felt in the air between them, air thick with tension
and fear. Helen had a crazy idea that if she could reach out
and gather the silence in her arms, she could somehow
destroy it and they would both breathe freely again.

He handed her a steaming cup without a word and placed
his mug on the table. He stoked the stove, every movement
evidence of his dejection. With slow deliberation, he drew on
his shirt and sat down, taking long gulps of the scalding
coffee.

'I don't know where, or how, to begin,' he rasped.

'Maria! For pity's sake, tell me about her link with us!'
cried Helen.

He made to reach out his hand and comfort her, but
frowned and clenched his fists instead.

'Maria!' he breathed. 'It always comes back to her! The
whole of my life had been shadowed by that woman!'

'Dimitri——' she wailed miserably, unable to bear the
suspense.

'Maria Zakro, as you know, lived in the valley. My father
took over the taverna when his parents died and he was quite
a young man. She was much younger than he was, but
incredibly beautiful, even as a young girl. As beautiful as
you,' he whispered harshly, raising tormented eyes to
Helen.

She bit back a sob. 'Was she like me?'

'Fairly. She was petite, curvy, brown-eyed—but with
black hair of course. Being blonde makes you look different.
And she had a particularly Cretan way of moving. But . . .
there is a similarity, now I know the connection.'

'How . . . is she your mother?' asked Helen tentatively.

'Hell, no!' he snapped, making her flinch with his
vehemence. 'Poor as Maria's parents were, they could
aspire to the young taverna owner as a son-in-law because of

her beauty. It was an unwritten agreement, but Maria grew
up with that idea, and my father got used to her following
him around like an adoring puppy. He was very handsome,
you see, strong and popular. But . . . well, I told you earlier
how he married my mother instead, and set the whole village
against him for reneging on his betrothal to Maria and
choosing money as his love.'

'That doesn't make . . .'

'Wait,' said Dimitri gently. 'We have the same father.'

'Dad? But . . .'

'Listen!' roared Dimitri, almost out of control. He ran his
hands through his hair at her fear and tried to get a grip on
himself.

'I'm sorry. I'm finding this difficult. More difficult than
you could ever know. You see, your mother was my father's
mistress. Agnes—my mother—told me. This was both
before and after his marriage. Because of Maria, my parents
never had a chance to make their marriage work. She was
always in the background, swinging her hips as she walked
the tracks, flaunting herself.'

'You can't be sure that's the truth!' blurted Helen.
'That's your mother's version!'

'True. But she enticed Father, nevertheless! After their
marriage, Father and Agnes worked their way around the
hotels, but Father came back to Vronda often, and my
mother believes he visited Maria frequently. I gather that,
after I was born, Father rarely touched my mother again.
He was finding comfort elsewhere.'

'Again, that's your mother's story——'

'And mine,' he said bitterly. 'I remember her, you know.
I was just a boy, but she took pity on me,' said Dimitri in a
remote voice. 'And in those days I didn't know the sort of
woman she was. I'd be walking the hills alone and come
across her watching her goats. She taught me the names of
flowers, the Cretan names, that is. Your mother loved

flowers, like you.'

'She was kind, to befriend you,' said Helen, picturing the withdrawn, solitary boy and her mother together.

'Very kind,' he said sardonically, making Helen's heart twist with pain. 'One day I picked some wild azalea for her. It was early and she wasn't in the downstairs room. I was thoughtless in my eagerness, innocent that I might intrude. She was living alone, I was only a little boy and privacy is not part of our culture. I ran up the steps to her bedroom and walked straight in.'

His voice had grown very quiet with the memory. Suddenly, Helen didn't want to know what he saw.

'Dimitri, you don't have to tell me these personal details,' she said nervously.

'I do, since you're part of the family,' he said bitterly. 'You have to know. You have to be convinced. Maria was there, rather as you were that night I took you to the Cretan Palace, standing in a simple white dress . . .' He bit his lip. 'The trouble was, Father was there too.'

'Dimitri!' she cried, her hand flying to her mouth. 'Was he . . . were they . . .'

'No,' he growled. 'They were not making love. They were both dressed. But they looked guilty; even at my tender age, I felt the waves of it reaching out to me. And it is unheard of for a man to enter a young woman's bedroom. I knew what they'd been doing, with the bed all unmade.'

'Did your father say anything?' whispered Helen.

'He told me quietly to get out and never to mention to my mother that I'd seen anything,' he said. 'Soon after that, Maria left the valley. I suppose Father thought it was a little dangerous, having her on his doorstep. Then she disappeared. Father found out that she was pregnant. Apparently Father went half out of his mind with guilt. Somewhere in the world was his child. You are that child. My father's daughter, my half-sister.' His voice was barely audible.

A flood of relief washed through Helen, making her tremble violently. Whatever had happened before, whatever relationship there had been between Dimitri's father and her own mother, he had made the wrong assumption.

'Dimitri, you're mistaken,' she said gently. 'Maybe most of that is true, maybe my mother was your father's mistress, but Dad did meet her in Agios Nikolaos, and *he* is my father. We have no parent in common.'

'Who says so? He does? Do you have any other evidence?'

'My birth certificate!'

'Helen, there's only one way Maria could stay for a long period in England without a work permit, and that is to claim an Englishman fathered her child.'

'But he did!'

'I doubt it. You see, she loved my father passionately.'

'But . . . surely,' she stumbled, half-frozen with horror. 'Why would he lie? Why . . . Oh!'

Dimitri gripped her arms tightly. 'So. You have thought of a reason, why he should pretend you are his daughter?' he rasped.

Her father—Dick—had deceived her about her mother for twenty-five years. Could he have done the same about himself? Was he still lying, so that he held on to her, worried that her real Cretan father would claim her? Helen gave a sob, inwardly convinced that Dimitri's story was true. It all made sense to her now.

'Very soon after I was born,' she said shakily, 'Dad had an accident that paralysed him. He couldn't father any children after that. Maybe . . .'

'Yes. Maybe he made things easier for Maria by allowing his own name to go on your birth certificate, and maybe he decided to continue the deception, to pretend you were his,' finished Dimitri. 'He loves you very much, yes?'

'Yes,' she whispered.

'Enough to lie so that he doesn't lose you?' pursued Dimitri relentlessly.

'I suppose so,' she said miserably. 'But I'm blonde! I've got his hair!' she cried suddenly, her eyes alive again.

'You could have inherited that through my father. My Kastelli grandmother was blonde. That proves nothing.'

'Oh, this is awful!' moaned Helen. 'I don't know who I am or where I am! My head is reeling. I'm trying to think logically, but no sense comes out. All that happens is this dreadful voice saying "who is your father?" I can't stand it!'

Dimitri's fingers began to stroke her arms in concern, but then he gave an irritable mutter and dropped his hands.

'I'm afraid it's clear who your father is, Helen,' he croaked. 'You see, my father's no fool. He's the most astute and careful man I know. So tell me this. If you're not his daughter, why on earth should he leave half his estate to you?'

'What?'

'No man would make a bequest like that to an unrelated child he'd never even seen. He must be convinced to leave such a vast inheritance to you. The fact that you share the Kastelli estate with me is proof enough.'

'I don't believe this!' breathed Helen, shaking her head. 'You're making it up. Why mention it now? Why not before?'

'I didn't want you to know,' he snapped. 'Like Father, I've been searching for Maria, but, unlike him, it wasn't to welcome her and tell her she was well cared for financially. I wanted to keep her away from him. I intended persuading Maria to agree to a cash settlement from me, instead of taking half the assets. I had no wish to share my inheritance with a woman who had ruined my parents' marriage and therefore my upbringing. How Maria could sleep with my father when he was married, I don't know.'

'Don't you think he had some say in the matter?' she said angrily.

'It's always the woman who makes the running. It's she who decides what is and what is not allowable,' he said harshly. 'Women have more control than men, and if they set out to seduce a man he doesn't have much chance.'

'That's the most . . .'

'*You* decided—thank God!—that *we* should not make love, not I,' he pointed out. 'You decided how far I could go. You had the control, I didn't.'

'Don't remind me!' she cried, aghast.

'I have to,' he retorted grimly. 'I have to keep reminding myself. Father has settled estates on you because you are his own flesh and blood, and we'd both do well to remember that fact. Obviously the affection I've felt for you was brotherly love, and I confused that with something else. Family affection isn't something I'm used to feeling,' he said wryly.

'I don't want any of the money,' said Helen quietly.

He looked at her in amazement.

'Millions of pounds' worth? Surely that would change your life and that of Dick Summers, the man who has brought you up?'

'Yes. And we're very happy with life as we have it, thank you.'

'Incredible! You don't understand yet, do you? Helen, you are virtually the owner of seven hotels and in control of huge budgets that are allocated to run them. Don't you think that will alter your life? Do you think Father will allow you to return to England and live with Dick Summers?'

'Oh! Dimitri, I don't want any of this! I want my normal, ordinary, happy life!' she wailed.

'Impossible. You have responsibilities now.'

'I'll give them to you,' she said quickly. 'You can have my half.'

'Oh, yes? Tell Father that and you'll kill him,' he said coldly. 'He's lived with the obsession of finding your mother or you and making some kind of recompense for the wrong he did her. He made sure her house was ready for when she returned. Every week he checked it to see that the woman who cleaned and aired it was doing her job well. Lately, since his stroke, I've had to take on that weekly check. You mustn't endanger his life. You mustn't ruin his chance to redeem himself before he dies, or to see his only daughter. You can't take that away from him.'

Helen began to weep quietly. With a groan, Dimitri took her in his arms and rocked her gently.

'Cry, sweetheart,' he murmured, his breath fanning her ear. 'Let it all out. I'm here to care for you. I'll help you to adjust.'

'I don't *want* to adjust!' she moaned, flinging her arms around his neck. 'I don't want you to be my brother!'

He let out a harsh breath. 'There isn't much we can do about that, Helen. We can't turn the clock back.'

'You ought to hate me,' she sobbed.

'I know. I did before I met you. I hated the child who had my father's unquestioning love. He gave me none, and would have given you everything. But . . . I can't hate you. Not at all. In a way, I wish I did, it would make things easier.'

'Can't we pretend we never met? Can't I go back home and be just as I was before?' she muttered into his neck.

Dimitri's hands stroked her slender shoulders. 'You can't do that—you *are* different, now you know. Besides, if we still appear to be tracing Maria's child when Father eventually dies, half the estate will be frozen. You'd be responsible, sweetheart, for destroying the business.'

Gently his hands and voice caressed her. Helen thought her mind would never cope with the implications of his revelations. She would have to meet his father—and his mother!

'Dimitri,' she said, her tear-stained face searching his. 'Your mother's going to be so upset! What will she think?'

He heaved a huge sigh. 'Father will be ecstatic, she will be horrified. We have to face it, though. Things have to take their natural course.'

'If only my mother hadn't been . . . ' She couldn't say the word, it stuck in her throat. To be the daughter of a woman who . . . Helen's eyes filled again.

'Don't blame her, Helen,' said Dimitri sympathetically, giving her shoulders an understanding squeeze. 'She was a passionate woman who felt safe in her belief that she would marry Father. When he married elsewhere, she had fallen in love too deeply to resist temptation. But I must admit that I find it hard to forgive her for not letting Father take responsibility for his own child. That's what wounded him so deeply.'

'But my father—I mean—oh, damn! She and Dick . . .'

He shrugged. 'Who's to know what happened there? From what I heard, Maria only had one love in her life. I doubt that she encouraged Dick Summers. I believe she was faithful to Father. This is why I'm convinced your father's story is a cover-up for the truth. Everyone here knows what she felt for Stavros Kastelli. I suspect that it was your father's kind heart—and perhaps a fatal fascination for Maria—that made him take pity on her and agree to accept paternity.'

'I understood that something in Crete held her, that she wanted to go back and pined for her home,' said Helen listlessly. 'I suppose it was your father she longed for.'

'Our father,' he reminded her quietly.

Helen shut her eyes and tried to control her shaky emotions. She'd never get used to the idea. The whole of her life was in turmoil.

'You were right, we *must* leave,' she muttered. 'It wasn't a lie about the helicopter, was it?'

'No. We use it ourselves, but often fly influential guests from place to place. It's in Cyprus.'

'When we were on the beach,' she said hesitantly, 'was it making a special journey?'

He nodded. 'An old friend of Father's had flown in. A national figure. It wasn't possible for you to be around—I couldn't risk questions. I didn't like deceiving you, Helen, but safety has been drummed into me and I had to be cautious and keep you in the dark. Now, of course,' he sighed, 'it's a different matter.'

'Now I'm family,' she said in a dull tone. 'Dimitri, I must ring home when we get away from here. I have to talk to . . . to . . . oh, I don't know what to call him now!'

'Gently, take it easy. Of course you must ring. The minute we reach my house,' he promised.

The thought of entering that cold palace made Helen shrink.

'Don't be afraid,' said Dimitri, sensing that. 'I will stand by you. No one will hurt you in any way.'

'Oh, Dimitri! I do love you so very much!' she cried, holding him as tightly as she could. Sisterly, she told herself. Sisterly, sisterly, *sisterly*!

'God!' he breathed, then his arms tightened around her like hard steel bands, and the breath was almost squeezed from her body before she was released. 'And I love you too, sweetheart.' He dropped a kiss on her cheek, his eyes strayed to her mouth, and his teeth tore savagely at his lower lip. 'So,' he said lightly, going over to make some more coffee. 'We will have love in the Kastelli family, after all!'

Helen's eyes filled with tears. They rolled down her cheeks unchecked as she watched every move he made, her heart aching. Her love for him swelled within her, refusing to be crushed; her desire to assuage his pain was equally strong. She wanted him to be happy. She would do anything to make him lose that tortured look, even accept

a different role in his life, though that would be a living hell
for her. No doubt the forbidden feelings she still harboured
would fade; it was because they hadn't known they had the
same father and had mistaken the deep bond of affection for
sexual love. Her brain and body were still muddled. Time
would erase the sensations she was experiencing now, and
they would be a united family.

The tears flowed on. She didn't *want* to be part of his
family! She *loved* him!

'Helen!' He stood unhappily, holding the mugs of coffee
in his hands, helpless in the face of her distress. 'Don't cry,
please! I can't bear to see you so miserable. Things will work
out. They'll get better, I promise. There's no way they can
be any worse.'

'No.' She suddenly slumped with utter exhaustion,
drained by the traumatic events. 'I'm so tired,' she said in a
small voice.

'That's good. Go to sleep. When you wake, we'll sort out
what we're going to do. I'll probably stay here to be with you
till you have had some breakfast, and then go down the
mountain to see if we can get you brought down on a
stretcher or something.' His mouth smiled wanly at her—a
brave try, but his eyes were dead. 'Don't worry about
anything. I'll look after you.'

'I know,' she whispered, her heart breaking. She turned
into the pillow and tried to stifle the sobs. Dimitri left her
alone to her misery till she had cried herself out, and then he
came over with a warm, moistened cloth and wiped her face
tenderly, then dried it. A light kiss brushed her forehead and
he sat stroking her hair. The last thing Helen remembered
before she slept was how much his hand trembled.

Now her small hand was trembling in his as he sat beside her
stretcher in the back of his pick-up van. Three tough-looking
Cretan men from the village had toiled up the mountain

path with him and brought her down, and one of them was
driving the truck for him.

They were zigzagging up the narrow road which led to his
house, and it looked even more forbidding to Helen as they
drew nearer. Without the comfort of Dimitri's hand, she
would have leapt out of the truck, sprained ankle and all,
and tried to run away. Her stomach was churning with ap-
prehension about her welcome. Despite the weakly filtering
sun, and the warm air, Dimitri's hand was icy: he was
apparently as nervous as she was.

The truck swept into a circular courtyard surrounded with
honeysuckle and exotic plants. They had driven through a
checkpoint, and been investigated by the dogs which roamed
loose around the estate.

Dimitri waved away all help. Carefully he lifted Helen
and walked up a long flight of steps, questioning one of the
hovering servants in Greek.

'Father's on the lower terrace,' he said to Helen.

She couldn't stop shaking. Dimitri eyed her anxiously.
They walked under a tunnel of magenta bougainvillaea,
glorious in the bright, dewy morning. The air was sweet
with the scent of roses, carnations, honeysuckle and
Madonna-lilies, and to Helen it seemed ironic that the world
was continuing as if their troubles didn't exist.

They came out on to a sweeping semi-circular terrace,
dotted with huge clay jars and specimen plants. The view
across to the snow-capped mountains beyond Dimitri's hide-
out was spectacular and took Helen's breath away. It seemed
that the newly washed sky hung clean and brilliant over the
jagged peaks, and the rapidly warming sun was beaming
down on the vast deep green landscape of the gorge.

Dimitri was taking her across the patio to a comfortable
arrangement of expensive sun-loungers. Over the back of a
long and deeply cushioned sofa, she saw the top of a man's
head. His father. *Her* father! A wave of dizziness overcame

her and she flung herself to hide in Dimitri's chest, and he walked with her around the sofa.

'Father.'

'Morning. Do you *have* to bring your playthings to show me?'

Crushed into Dimitri's body, Helen clenched her teeth at the cruel insult, hating the way Dimitri had flinched in pain. Without a word, he placed her gently on a lounger facing his father, detaching her desperately clinging fingers from his neck with some difficulty.

'Don't leave me!' she cried, her eyes huge.

He sat close beside her and took her hand firmly.

'I have some good news for you,' he said to his father without expression.

Stavros Kastelli's eyes swept over Helen's dishevelled figure in derision. 'Not marriage, I hope?' he muttered.

Dimitri's chest inflated. 'No, Father. Prepare yourself for a shock. I want you to stay very calm, because what I'm going to say to you will come as a great surprise.'

Helen stared at the man who looked so bitter and unbending. She had to remember that in a moment he was going to have his world turned upside-down, too.

'Go on.' Stavros's alert eyes had narrowed speculatively.

'This, Father, is Helen. She is Maria Zakro's daughter.'

The change in his father's features was remarkable. Suddenly, he had softened, become vulnerable, as his shocked eyes gazed into Helen's and then examined her in increasing agitation.

'Proof!' The word came from his lips as soft as a breath.

'We have that. There is no doubt. Tell him the story, Helen,' prompted Dimitri.

Uncertainly, her voice cracking with emotion, she did so, totally unnerved by the almost desperate longing on Stavros's face. Dimitri had been right to make her come. This was obviously a wonderful moment for Stavros. He would be able to put right the wrong he did to her mother.

'I can't believe it!' he whispered.

'Are you all right? Do you want your pills?' asked Dimitri anxiously.

Helen realised how painful it must be for him to witness the love that Stavros was directing towards her, and her heart wept for Dimitri. And yet, despite all that, he cared for his father—and her. He was a big man in every way, she thought longingly.

'No.' Slowly, Stavros heaved himself out of the chair, and came over to Helen. He looked overjoyed. 'Maria's child,' he said in wonder, taking Dimitri's vacated seat. His hand reached out to touch her as if she might vanish. 'At last.' A huge, beaming smile lit his face, and Helen saw the likeness between him and Dimitri. 'You've made me very happy, Helen, to have seen you before I die. Helen! She has given you a Greek name! And what of her? Where is she?' he asked eagerly.

She and Dimitri exchanged glances.

'I'm afraid Maria died a long time ago, Father,' he said softly.

The big man's face crumpled and he couldn't speak for a moment. 'I always hoped . . . I wanted to have her forgiveness,' he said brokenly. 'Helen, I've made arrangements to atone for my unforgivable behaviour——'

'I've told her, Father.'

'What? You have? But . . . you were always against Maria and her child!' declared Stavros in surprise. 'I thought you'd keep the inheritance a secret from this sweet girl I love already, have always loved in my heart.'

He gazed fondly at Helen and her heart warmed to him. He had so much in material wealth and nothing of value emotionally. Now that could change, and with it the atmosphere in this chilling grandeur. She gave him a trembling smile.

'Blood must be thicker than water,' said Dimitri huskily.

'Perhaps,' said his father cryptically. 'Now, Helen, you must tell me all about yourself. Where you live and what you do, the things you like—and how Dimitri found you!'

'Father, you will go easily, won't you?' worried Dimitri.

'I feel wonderful. I have a new lease of life,' he smiled. 'Son, I know what it has meant to you, bringing Helen here. I'm aware that my life had been soured by regret and you have suffered. You suffer now, too, because I am angry that I can't work any more. I can't tell you how much it means to me that you didn't try to keep me in ignorance of Helen's existence. I shall never be able to thank you enough.'

Dimitri's eyes were bright as they looked at his happy father. 'It's odd, isn't it,' he said quietly, 'that once you experience love, it can spread to embrace everyone around you? And you may not realise it yet, but your gentleness and delight with Helen seems to have spilled over to me. You haven't barked at me for some minutes,' he added wryly.

Stavros laughed, and so did Helen. If she brought father and son together, then she must be happy. Or must she?

CHAPTER TWELVE

'GOOD morning, Helen.' Every morning for the last ten days, Helen had seen the light of joy on Stavros's face and it had given her deep pleasure. He could be an irascible old man, but she seemed to bring out the best in him.

'Morning, Stavros.' She kissed both his cheeks affectionately. He'd quite understood that she found it difficult to call him 'father' and that she felt that was betraying the man who had brought her up so lovingly. Stavros didn't mind: Helen's presence was enough.

The only thing that bothered her was that she hadn't been able to speak to Dick: after ringing a neighbour, she'd discovered that he'd been so lonely without her that he'd gone to stay with a friend who had no telephone. Feeling worried that she hadn't spoken with him, she left a message that he was to contact her urgently, the moment he got back home.

'Good morning, Agnes,' she smiled, and on impulse bent to touch the elegant woman's cheekbones with hesitant lips. But Agnes didn't recoil, as she had half expected. She gave Helen a brief nod in greeting, and a relieved Helen made her way to the chair which was being held out for her by Manilos.

'Have we got some of that lovely yoghurt and honey this morning?' she asked him hopefully.

'Yes, Miss Helen.' The stiffly formal Cretan manservant had unbent considerably under the force of Helen's happy friendliness. 'Cook made extra croissants, too,' he said indulgently.

'Oh!' Helen clapped an embarrassed hand to her mouth

while Stavros laughed.

'Can't have you staring wistfully at the empty plate like yesterday,' grinned Stavros.

'I find these wonderful breakfasts hard to resist,' sighed Helen, choosing a dish of wild strawberries from the cornucopia of fruit arranged in the centre of the table. 'I think it has something to do with the surroundings. They make me think I'm on a picnic, and I *always* eat non-stop on them, because I'm refuelling after long walks.'

'Don't apologise, my dear,' smiled Stavros. 'We like to see a healthy appetite. Tell us about these walks in Madeira, and what you had to do in your research.'

As Helen ate and chattered, she wondered at the ability of human beings to adapt. Here she was, wrapped in luxury, sitting on the edge of a spectacular hillside in the bright sunshine with an incomparable view spreading before her. Choughs wheeled and fought in the air above them, eagles and griffon vultures dotted the thinner atmosphere over the Thripti peaks, while little finches sang in the thick foliage around them.

Mrs Kastelli was drinking her usual mixture of champagne and orange juice, Stavros his delicate blend of China tea, while Helen sipped orange so fresh that she'd seen Koula—one of the maids—picking the fruit a few minutes earlier!

At first, Agnes had been as cold and unwelcoming as an ice wall. But Helen's immobility had helped—it made her more vulnerable and less threatening. Agnes was hardly friendly, but had lost her original hostility. It seemed to Helen that Stavros became more and more affectionate and considerate towards Agnes as the days progressed, as though he understood how difficult the situation was for her and as if he wanted to make things easier.

Agnes loved Stavros deeply, that was clear from the way she had begun to respond to his gentle concern. And that, too, made the atmosphere less tense. Then, of course, Helen's natural exuberance and easy, unstilted behaviour had made it difficult for Agnes to be rude. There was a long way to go yet, Helen knew that, but she could see some kind of eventual coming to terms with the situation as far as she and Agnes were concerned.

'Helen sounds an asset to any business, don't you think so, my dear?' Stavros asked Agnes.

'Very efficient.'

Her tone was crisp, but she smiled when Stavros patted her hand gratefully, and Helen saw that once she must have been a striking woman. The lines of bitterness disappeared when she smiled, to reveal a softer, loving woman beneath. Helen kept her fingers crossed that Stavros would continue to show his wife this tender care.

'What do you think you'll do now?' he asked. 'Will you give in your notice?'

'No,' said Helen, shaking her head emphatically, and then, as Dimitri walked on to the terrace, she felt her stomach plummet. He wore a short-sleeved, crisp white shirt with an open collar and pale gold trousers, beautifully cut with casual shoes to match. Helen's heart thumped in her ribcage. He looked so dark, so tanned and handsome. A really good-looking half-brother, she told herself.

He greeted both his parents with a kiss, but not Helen. To her he merely gave a brief, unsmiling nod.

'Helen's just telling us that she's going to carry on working,' said Stavros.

Dimitri sat down and didn't look up from the stuffed courgettes he was picking at morosely. When he failed to respond to his father's remark, Helen broke the uneasy silence.

'I thought about it and decided it was better that I should do something I was good at, rather than enter the hotel business,' she said, hoping for his approval.

'How about setting up walks or donkey trails for our hotel guests all over the world?' suggested Dimitri, still concentrating on his food.

'That's a lovely idea!' beamed Helen enthusiastically. Then her face fell. 'But . . . I'd want to do that as part of my present job. I couldn't leave, I'd be letting John down. He relies on me.'

'This is your boss?' asked Stavros.

Helen nodded. 'He's been so kind, almost like a . . .' She laughed. 'So many fathers to look after me!'

'You can't blame us,' said Stavros. 'You must either attract the fathering instinct in men or the Romeo urge. Don't you agree, Dimitri?'

He shrugged, the lines of his face cold and hard. 'Excuse me,' he said, rising from the table. 'I have a plane to catch.'

'You haven't eaten anything!' cried Agnes.

'Plane? Where? Where are you going?' asked Helen, upset.

'Seychelle islands.'

'There's no problems there I know of,' said his father, puzzled. 'If anything, you ought to be here. It's coming up to Easter and . . .'

'I can't stay,' he said. 'I'll miss the flight.' His eyes shifted and he looked at Helen for the first time since his arrival. 'When are you leaving?'

'Leaving? She's not leaving!' cried Stavros.

Helen floundered. She ought to go home to find Dick. He had to know what was happening. She ought to sort things out with John, and she ought to talk to Dimitri about her future.

'I—I was going to talk to you today about . . .'

'Talk to Father,' he interrupted curtly. 'Make any arrangements you have to. After I've arrived in the Seychelles, I'll ring him and find out what you plan to do. I don't expect I'll see you much in future: I'm ending my holiday.'

'You were going to take some time off . . .' began Agnes.

'Yes. I find I need to return to work,' he said coldly.
'Goodbye, Helen. See you later, Mother, Father.'

'But . . . but . . .' Helen's mind was refusing to function.
All she could think of was that Dimitri's behaviour was very
odd and he was giving the impression that they might not see
each other again. Over the last few days he had become pro-
gressively more reclusive and difficult to talk to, answering
in monosyllables and doing his best not to be near her. It
seemed that he *was* jealous, and that he *did* hate the idea of
her ousting him from the sole inheritance. It was terrible to
be hated by someone you . . . you had a family affection for,
she thought sadly.

'You will be here for Easter,' said Stavros sternly.

'Not this year, Father. I don't think . . .'

'Yes!' Everyone jumped as Stavros banged on the table.

'Careful, you'll excite yourself,' warned Dimitri.

'You're damn right I will!' Stavros cried. 'For the first
time our family is united and we can have the best Easter
we've ever had in our lives, and you decide that work is
more important! Dimitri! Don't make the mistake I made!
You *will* come home for the festival or I'll . . . I'll . . .'

'Please!' Dimitri placed soothing hands on his father's
shoulders. Stavros was flushing an unhealthy red. 'I—oh,
dammit! All right. I'll be home. Now I must leave. 'Bye.'

After breakfast, Helen walked down to the village,
refusing transport, even though Stavros was going there.
She explained that the short walks she had taken recently
had shown that her ankle was healed, and she wanted to
enjoy meandering along the valley track. She needed time to
think, too.

Once in the village, she made for the tiny general shop
that had been created from a front room. She'd heard that
Easter candles were being sold there, and she wanted to
choose some for her room. Greeting the four villagers packed

in the confined space, she gazed in awe at the long, colourful
candles with their matching streamers. One of the women
helped her to untangle the ones she had selected, and then
began the pantomime of payment and discussing the weather.
Helen's Greek was still very limited and she wanted to take
lessons. There was so much to think of and to do!

Clutching her parcel and taking her leave, she stepped
outside to see people busily whitewashing everything in
sight: houses, telegraph poles, the post that held the
loudspeaker to warn villagers of disasters, trees, kerbs . . .
everything! Filled with delight at the sight, she put down her
candles and gestured to a grey-haired woman of about
seventy, who was trying to paint a mulberry tree. With some
doubt in her dark eyes, the woman handed Helen the brush
and she began to slap paint on happily.

Stavros appeared, being helped down the steps by a
smiling Agnes. They were deep in conversation with each
other and Helen was glad to see the change in the woman.

'Hello!' she called happily, waving the brush.

'Integrating already,' grinned Stavros.

'Absolutely,' she agreed. 'Hold the tin for me, so I can
reach the higher bits, will you?'

Agnes started at Helen's innocent request, and her eyes
widened when Stavros chuckled and did as he was told.

'Have a coffee, my dear,' he told his wife. 'This could
take some time.'

'Will you be all right?'

His arm reached out and lay reassuringly on her shoulder.
'I'll be fine. I refuse to have another heart attack. I have too
much to make up for.' His eyes begged Agnes'
understanding.

She looked at Helen, frowning intently in concentration.
'I never thought I'd feel anything but hate for her,' she
whispered in Greek.

'I've been a bastard,' replied Stavros in the same

language. 'And a fool.'

'Higher,' complained Helen. 'I can't reach the tin.'

Stavros grinned at Agnes. 'Go and sit in the shade, my love. We'll talk later.'

Time passed so quickly that Helen was astonished when Stavros suggested they had something to eat since it was nearly three o'clock! They had worked as a giggling team, moving to help finish the walls of the church while the old priest—who wore his hair in a bun and sported a pair of sunglasses—contentedly watched them as he sipped his ouzo and chatted to Agnes. Helen was pleased to notice that the villagers were friendly towards her now—and not so wary of Stavros. No one could be, she thought, looking at his relaxed and gentle face, splattered with limewash. Dimitri was so like him. A stab of pain shot through her. That was the only sad thing about her new situation—that and the fact that Dick would be upset to know she'd found out he was not her real father. But he wouldn't suffer. She would love him as much and be with him as much—somehow. Dimitri was different. It was something she had to keep pushing to the back of her mind because, if she dwelled on it, waves of misery engulfed her and the new-found pleasures were ashes in her mouth. Her life would be a tragedy if she allowed her ruthlessly suppressed feelings to surface.

She had to forget what he had meant to her. If only she could reach Dick! Until she did, Helen knew that the story would only be half told and half understood. They must all meet and talk. Dick must tell her what had really happened, and then it would all be clear to her and she could begin to shape her new life.

Dimitri returned. He was more tanned and more reserved than before. Helen hardly saw him. It seemed he ate little, and Agnes was worried that he was taking the stringencies of Lent too far.

Helen had been asked to stay till after Easter, and if she hadn't been able to contact Dick then she was to fly to England and try to find out where he might have gone.

She felt increasingly miserable. She had everything she could possibly ask for in the world, and yet there was a terrible emptiness in her life. How could there ever be a man who matched up to her brother?

On the evening of Good Friday, they all drove to the tiny village church, Dimitri sitting right against the car door and staring fixedly out of the window. He bit off anyone's head when they addressed a remark to him.

'You're so bad-tempered at the moment!' exclaimed Agnes after one irritable exchange.

'You wanted me here for Easter and I'm here. Don't expect anything else,' he growled.

Helen bit her lip. She did want it to be a lovely family get-together. Her hand reached out to touch his arm tentatively, and he pushed it away with a ferocious expression on his face.

'Don't do that,' he gritted.

'Why do you hate me?' she whispered quietly, her eyes full of tears.

'Why shouldn't I?' he seethed, turning his broad back to her.

Helen leaned back and stared sightlessly out of the window. This was the price they'd paid, then. It seemed that you could never be fully happy. Something always marred your life. She would give anything to be back on Paradise island with him, with hardly a care in the world.

They joined the procession which trailed around the village streets, led by the old priest swinging a silver censer, his golden robes glittering in the light of the giant candles carried by his acolytes.

Women tossed blossom on the ground in front of the priest, and the air was heavy with its scent as dozens of feet crushed the fragrant blooms. People spoke in hushed tones and the slow, heavy beat of the mournful drums reached into Helen's soul and depressed her usual high spirits. Why couldn't she accept being Dimitri's sister? Why was she confusing sisterly love with sexual love?

If only Stavros hadn't got Maria pregnant! If only . . . Helen stumbled and Dimitri's hand caught her. For a brief moment she felt his strength, the power of his chest and the hardness of his hip as he drew her to him with an involuntary movement. But when he had steadied her firmly on her feet, he quickly strode on ahead. He stayed with an old woman, helping her tenderly and with great charm, as the procession wound its way up the stepped streets and into the church. During the sad service, with the priest's rich bass vibrant with feeling ringing in her ears, Helen surreptitiously watched Dimitri standing at the front of the church with his father. She couldn't see much: his proud, dark neck and the wide stretch of his shoulders in the tailored black suit, was everything to Helen.

She came away very thoughtful. She *had* to talk to Dick. If only he would telephone! She'd left the number and every day she awaited his call. She couldn't allow herself to feel like this about Dimitri. She must have confirmation of the truth.

In the house, the tension was mounting. What had been a relaxed, open atmosphere without Dimitri had became fraught with fraying tempers. And Agnes had made some odd remark to Helen, asking her how she and Dimitri had got on before he discovered they were relatives. Helen's fumbled answer seemed to do little to satisfy Agnes's growing alarm at the hostility existing between them now.

Just before midnight on the Easter Sunday, Helen stood next to Agnes once more in the church that was

crowded with the worklined, proud and vigorous villagers
with their round-eyed children. Everything was in pitch
darkness. There was a muttering, a fidgeting and then the
priest appeared from the little sanctuary holding three
lighted candles.

Helen knew that he was telling the congregation to
come and receive the light, and the back of her neck
prickled as lighted tapers were passed to the priest and
every candle in the church was lit. Midnight struck,
'Christ is Risen' was sung with heart-wrenching
sweetness and she saw Dimitri turn and give her such a
look of profound longing that she began to tremble. The
bells pealed joyously and Helen's heart was so full that she
couldn't move when the rest of the people filed out of the
church. Dimitri had seen her standing in the pew,
transfixed by him, and he too had not moved. Then,
unable to bear the agony of his eyes any longer, she gave a
low moan, turned and hurried out, trying to shield her
candle and keep it alight. If she could get it home without
it going out, she would have good luck. And that was
what she needed right now.

Outside, the sky was bright with an exuberant display
of fireworks. Everyone was shouting at the tops of their
voices and kissing . A little red dyed hard-boiled egg was
thrust into her hand by Stavros.

'Come on, Dimitri,' he called. 'Stop lurking in the
doorway.' He pulled his son next to Helen. 'Crack the
egg with Helen and give the kiss of love, you renegade,
you!' His tone was affectionate but commanding.

Dimitri's teeth snagged his lip. Without looking at
Helen, he cracked his egg against hers and began to peel it
with impatient fingers.

'You forgot the kiss!' Stavros yelled, pushing him to
Helen.

Miserably she looked up at Dimitri. Their eyes locked

and they stared at each other, the raw misery tearing up
from their very souls. Gritting his teeth, he bent his head
briefly and his cold lips touched her flushed cheek for
what seemed the first time in an eternity. Helen clutched
at his arms and, with an outrush of breath, Dimitri held
her to him.

'It's all right, sweetheart,' he muttered, his hands
pressing hard into her spine. 'We'll work something out.
Give me time. I need to adjust to the different situation.'

'I thought you hated me,' she said, a catch in her voice,
and holding on to him for all she was worth.

'No. Just myself. Forgive me, little . . . sister.'

Helen winced at the word that was wrenched from him.

'Come on,' called Stavros. 'Time for the feast.'

'Oh, God!' muttered Dimitri, pulling away and disappearing into the crowd.

Helen stayed a moment to gather herself together, and
then felt she was being watched. She looked up to see an
alarmed expression on Agnes's face.

Despite the late hour—or rather early, since it was the
morning already—everyone was returning to their homes
for the feast. Stavros had laid on a wonderful supper and
invited all the village, so tables and chairs had been set out
on the cascading terraces of his house and garlands of
blossom hung overhead. The dark night was lit by
hundreds of candles. Helen's own candle had lasted all
the way home, but she couldn't see where her good luck
would come from. The situation seemed hopeless.

The worst part was that she had to sit next to Dimitri.
All through the meal of traditional Cretan dishes, she was
overwhelmingly aware of his body, vibrant, alive, un-
touchable. He wasn't her half-brother, he couldn't be.
Helen held back the knifing pains that pierced her body.
She had to keep telling herself that he *was*, he *was*!

He didn't talk to her at all. They both made bright talk

to everyone else instead, neither doing much more than pick at the aromatic lamb with its egg and lemon sauce, and Helen didn't even want her favourite roast potatoes, sprinkled with wild mountain oregano.

The dancing began. Stavros and Agnes led it, Stavros a rose behind his ear for the pleasure of its scent. Helen noticed that many men had tucked roses or carnations behind their ears. Cretan men were highly sensual, she thought with a pang. Dimitri hadn't followed the custom. She was forced to take the floor with him, for the sake of appearances. All the Kastellis together: a happily united family!

By now, Helen's desperate misery was total. The notes of the *bouzouki* mingled with the delicate strings of the *luta* and *lyra* as she moved numbly in Dimitri's arms. He held her awkwardly, unused to dancing at such a polite distance from a woman.

The floor became crowded, as laughing villagers joined them. They were jostled constantly by the elated people, who were merry on the lashings of *ouzo* and *raki* and the raw village wine. Dimitri was forced to protect Helen by drawing her to him. Life leapt in Helen's body: a wild pulsating heat that slowed her steps and made her brain stop functioning.

'Keep moving, damn you!' grated Dimitri.

To her astonishment, she noticed that she was actually standing still and they were both swaying gently to the music. Her huge brown eyes lifted to his hard, bitter face.

'You're *not* my half-brother!' she whispered in a cracked voice. 'You're *not!*'

Dimitri thrust her furiously away, his face working with uncontainable emotions, and then he was forcing a pathway through the startled dancers, blindly, ruthlessly pushing them aside without pausing to see the results of his actions.

Helen fought for air. She saw how frightened Agnes looked, then the faces all round her turned into blurs and she slid to the ground in a dead faint.

CHAPTER THIRTEEN

WHEN she came to, the first thing Helen saw the worried faces of Dimitri's parents. And that was how she thought of them now: *nothing* would convince her that she had the same blood as Dimitri.

'Helen, are you all right?' asked Stavros anxiously. 'My God, if that son of mine has treated you cruelly, I'll make him regret the day!'

'Hush, Stavros,' said Agnes. 'The problem is greater than you think. Isn't it, Helen? I have an idea what it is about.'

She nodded miserably. 'I—I want to ask you some questions,' she said to Stavros.

'I thought as much. In that case, I'll see if I can trace Dimitri,' muttered Agnes.

'You won't say anything to him? You won't do anything . . .' Helen sat up quickly, afraid that Agnes might speak unkindly to him. It wasn't his fault, after all.

Agnes shook her head. 'I love him too, you know. I only want to prevent him from doing something stupid. He's in such a state he could harm himself,' she said, and left quickly.

Helen bit her lip. She badly wanted to search for Dimitri too and make sure he was all right, but she *had* to sort this out first.

Stavros sat down close to her. 'So, what's worrying you? It's not . . . Helen, you aren't pregnant, are you? some boyfriend at home . . .'

'No!' she cried in protest. 'I haven't . . . I mean . . .'

He patted her hand. 'It's all right. I understand. What is it, then? I thought you were happy, and only concerned that you hadn't told your father about us yet.'

'You said "your father",' she said, suddenly alert.

Stavros dropped his eyes. 'So I did,' he muttered.

Helen caught hold of his hands and willed him to look at her. 'Stavros, you *must* tell me, it's so important! You're not my father, are you?'

He stared back helplessly. 'I never said I was,' he answered.

'Thank God!' A huge load was lifted from Helen's shoulders and her spirits began to lift, to soar. She could love Dimitri!

'Helen!'

She threw her arms around Stavros Kastelli's neck. 'Oh, I didn't mean it like that!' she cried, hugging him tightly. 'I love you dearly, you know that. The thing is, I also love Dimitri.'

'Well, of course, you . . .' His eyes became intent. 'You mean *love*?' he queried.

'I mean *love*,' she agreed, her eyes alight with joy. 'I love him so much, Stavros, you can't *know* how much. And I'm sure he loves me. When we thought . . .' Her eyes shut briefly at the painful feelings she had experienced. 'I'm going to find out for sure. It could only be desire,' she added, suddenly worried.

'Now I understand Dimitri's odd behaviour! Agnes knew. She realised. She must have wondered what you two were up to. Why didn't I see that, too? Helen, I—oh, dear! I've almost ruined two more lives, haven't I?'

'But why should you insist that Maria had borne you a daughter?' cried Helen.

Stavros heaved a huge sigh. 'I had to. It was the only way they would—however grudgingly—accept my decision to leave half the estate to Maria or her heirs.

They wouldn't have understood why I wanted to look after her: they would have contested my will and said I was insane.'

'But I don't understand *why* you wanted to give your money away, or what your relationship was with Maria.'

'Helen, she was a very beautiful child—I always saw her as one and couldn't desire her, however much I tried. She loved me and trusted me implicitly, and I let her down badly when I married Agnes instead.'

'Did you . . . did you love Agnes?' asked Helen shakily.

'Yes,' he said with another sigh. 'Yet my head was full of excitement at the thought of the challenge ahead of me. Agnes thought that Maria came between us. Not true. It was my ambition that did that. She became harsh and jealous. I denied her accusations that Maria was my mistress, but she would never believe me.'

'Dimitri told me he saw you both together,' she said in a low voice.

'It was the first and only time I'd visted her. I had gone to say that she must leave, for the sake of my marriage. Only that would convince Agnes that there was nothing between us. I offered Maria money to settle elsewhere, but she said all she wanted was me. But she left.'

'That turned Dimitri against you,' said Helen.

'Yes. But I couldn't explain, he wouldn't have understood. He was too young and I didn't have that kind of relationship with him. He was such a serious, withdrawn boy. A loner. He seemed so scornful of me. I couldn't express what I felt inside in case I was rejected,' explained Stavros. 'I'd been so wrapped up in the business that I hardly ever saw him, and never knew what to say when we were together.'

'He doesn't know that you love him,' said Helen gently.

'He will,' promised Stavros.

'How did you know Maria was pregnant?' asked Helen, with a sudden fear.

'One day I glimpsed her in the taverna in Agios Nikolaos and the next time I was there she'd gone. The manager told me she was pregnant. It was nothing to do with me, I swear to you on my son's head. You know the rest: she apparently went to your father and asked for help. I vowed that I would find her. You see, I felt guilty because I'd driven her to take refuge in another man's arms. It was my fault she'd tried to find love and affection elsewhere and ended up in trouble.'

'You can't hold yourself responsible!' cried Helen.

'I do. It may be irrational, but I do. And I had money by then, enough to help her. As the years went on, my guilt grew worse. I had to make some recompense to assuage my guilt—it became a matter of honour, so that eventually the Kastellis could hold their heads up high in the Vronda valley again. You can't imagine how terrible it is to be scorned by your old friends and neighbours. Until I made amends, we would be damned by the people. It was hard to see the way Dimitri had been rejected by everyone because of my actions so long ago. Cretan memories are long: vengeance is harsh.'

'Poor darling,' said Helen gently. 'You've suffered—you've all suffered. But,' she said, her eyes glistening with excitement 'I'm going to stop all that! Oh, Stavros, we're all going to be so happy! You and Agnes, Dad, Dimitri and me.'

'Excuse me, sir,' said Manilos, appearing in the doorway. 'There is a telephone call for Miss Helen.'

'Dad!' she cried, flying to the phone.

'Helen?' came his familiar tones. 'Are you all right? Is something . . .'

'No, I'm fine,' she cried. 'Listen, I've met people who knew my mother. I—oh, this is so difficult on the phone!'

she wailed.

'Calm down,' laughed Dick. 'I thought you were in trouble.'

'I was,' she said. 'Dad, I don't know how to ask this, but it is *vital*. Are you absolutely certain that you're my father?'

'What?'

'Please! It's important!'

'I'm certain. You see . . . I was the first.'

'You—oh, Dad, I'm so happy!' she cried, bursting into tears. Stavros took the phone from her, cradling her against his chest and began to speak. Helen recovered a little and was just wiping her eyes when Agnes came in, looking worried. She beckoned Helen over.

'Dimitri has gone!'

'Gone? Gone where?' cried Helen, her world crashing about her.

'I've no idea. His apartment looks like a bomb has hit it: clothes flung everywhere, personal items scattered in all directions. Yet none of the cars have gone and the night-shift guards say they haven't seen him: he's vanished into the darkness!'

'I know where he is,' said Helen in excitement. 'I know! I'll go to him.'

'It's still dark, Helen . . .'

'By the time I've got ready, it'll be almost dawn. Don't worry about me, I'll be all right. Nothing would stop me now, anyway,' she cried, her face glowing with eagerness.

Stavros broke off from his conversation with Dick. 'You're going to him? Take care,' he said softly. 'Give Dimitri my love—if you remember, that is,' he grinned wickedly. 'Tell him to be happy.'

'I will,' she promised, hugging him and a surprised Agnes.

*　　*　　*

High on the terraces, across the gorge, Helen could hear
and see the feasting and dancing. She smiled and pushed
on, working her way up the narrow mountain trail, glad
of her warm track suit in the chilly early morning. Lissos
finally came into sight, and she moved cautiously over the
narrow ridge with its precipitous drop on either side. A
light glimmered in the refuge hut, making her steps
lighter and her heart thud with anticipation.

It only added to her intense disappointment then, to
find that he was not there. A candle guttered low in a dish
and the stove had been lit but was now out. Her eyes
caught a small rucksack in the corner of the room. It must
be Dimitri's, please let it be his, she pleaded, hoping this
was her promised good luck.

She left her own bag there and went outside into the
crisp, clean air, clambering up over the ancient ruins,
searching for Dimitri. And there she found him, a short
distance away, his back to her, dressed in the same black
leather trousers and jacket as on the day she had first met
him.

At once her body turned to jelly with nerves. She was
assuming a lot, putting all his reactions, words and
behaviour together and convincing herself he loved her.
Sickness hit her stomach. She could be wrong, very
wrong, but she had to find out.

He sat absolutely still, sitting on a high rock where the
mountain fell away a thousand feet, staring into the
distant, sapphire Aegean without seeing anything at all.
Instead of the proudly held, magnificent strength that she
associated with his body, she had the illusion that he was
emptied of all life.

Helen almost yelled at him in exhilaration, wanting to
end his misery, then realised he'd probably fall in shock if
she did. Her heart aching for his grief, she quietly turned
and made her way back to the hut. First, she lit the stove

and drew out the bacon and sausages she had brought, placing them in a pan. When they were sizzling, she began to make a great deal of noise, banging furniture around and clanging saucepans. She laid the table and ran to the window.

He was coming! Striding with his wonderful, graceful fluid walk, his eyes alert as he wondered which shepherd had invaded his temporary private retreat. Helen could hardly breathe. Her pulses raced, the blood roaring in her ears. It was unbelievably difficult, restraining the urge to run to him and leap into his arms. Then she heard the door open, and his horrified gasp.

'Bacon and sausages all right?' she said casually. 'I forgot the eggs—I was in a bit of a rush.'

'Get out!' he growled.

'Don't talk to your future wife in that manner,' she said calmly.

'You bitch!'

She shot a nervous glance over her shoulder to find that he was gripping the door-post with whitening hands.

'You do know how to tear the knife . . .' he began.

'No knife, Dimitri,' she said softly, putting down the spatula in her hand and facing him. Oh, God! How terrifying he looked! His dark brows had met in a ferocious scowl and his eyes were slits of black ice. The whole of his body quivered from the battle going on within him. 'Did you ever notice that your father avoided calling me his child, his daughter? I've spoken to him. He swears that he never made love to Maria. I've spoken to Dick, my father. When he met her, she was a virgin. Your father had nothing to do with her pregnancy.'

'But . . .' He passed a shaking hand over his face. 'You mean . . .'

Helen felt her heart lurch. 'I mean Dick and Maria are my parents and Stavros and Agnes are yours. We have a

different father and a different mother. I do hope that's
crystal-clear. We are not related. Do you like your bacon
crisp?' she said, her voice rising an octave, despite her
efforts. The next few moments could make or break her
life.

'To hell with the bacon!' he yelled, striding towards
her.

'Oh,' she said nervously, backing away. 'The macho
approach again, is it?'

He stood in front of her, his chest heaving, looking
unnervingly virile and supremely male. 'You bet your
sweet life it is,' he growled.

'I——'

He ignored Helen's squeak and took the pan off the
heat.

'We are not related,' he said in an even tone.

'No!' she squeaked again, every nerve in her body
strung taut. *Would he never do anything?*

'Are you *sure*?'

'Oh, damn you, Dimitri! Your father swears that he
never touched my mother.'

'I'll kill him!' he breathed.

'No, you won't,' she said in a matter-of-fact tone.
'He's only just discovering that he can show love for
Agnes, and he wants the opportunity to show his love for
you. You can't kill him. He hasn't had the chance to be a
grandfather yet. So, what are you going to do about it?'
Her small chin tipped up belligerently, challenging him.

A slow smile crossed Dimitri's face. 'What am I going
to do? This.'

He held out his arms and Helen walked into them,
laying her head against his violently beating heart. For a
long time he just held her while their emotions took over.

'I felt so terrible,' he whispered eventually. 'So
confused. Every drop of my blood flowed faster when you

were near. Every nerve sprang alive. You had reached my
heart and brought me into the world of lovers. I can't tell
you how shattered I was to hear that you were my sister!'

'I never really believed it,' said Helen. 'I tried, very
hard, but I was sure I couldn't feel such wicked,
scandalous thoughts about you if we were related.'

He grinned and leaned back a little to look at her.
'Wicked? Scandalous? Tell me some of them,' he
murmured.

Helen felt her body liquefy. 'Why . . . talk?' she pouted
suggestively.

'Helen!'

All his loving and longing were contained in that one
word. As Helen's knees sagged from weakness, he swept
her up and carried her to the bed.

. 'Your father said I had to find time to tell you he loved
you very much,' she said shakily. 'And you were to be
happy.'

'I am,' he answered, wonderingly stroking her face as if
seeing her for the first time. 'I have never been happier.
Life is suddenly wonderful. We will make a wonderful life
for your father, too, If he doesn't want to lose his friends
and live here permanently, perhaps he'd like to spend the
winters with us. What do you think?'

'I think he'd love that,' she smiled. 'And I could carry
on working . . .'

'Till you want to begin a family,' he murmured.

'A family?' She laughed. 'You haven't proposed yet.'

'No. You did, I think, a few minutes ago.'

'Oh!' She hid her face in embarrassment, but her
hands were gently prised away.

'You will marry me, then?' he asked softly.

'You—you will have control of your father's bequest to
me then won't you?' Helen held her breath. How could
she be certain of his love? After all, his father had married

for ambition.

'Why should that matter?' Dimitri's fingers were feathering her ears and sending incredibly fierce messages to her body.

'Be-because he's still leaving half to me, and when you marry me it'll all go to you. You could be marrying me to make sure you're the sole boss,' she said tremulously, unable to believe that he loved her for herself alone. She was too ordinary, too . . .

'That is the *custom* of my country, not the law,' laughed Dimitri. 'Am I hearing correctly? Is this pushy, exuberant, confident, assertive and unbelievably stubborn woman suggesting that I might only find her bank balance and share power of interest?'

Helen's big eyes stared at him seriously.

Dimitri threw back his head and roared with laughter, while Helen grew more agitated. Finally she could stand it no longer.

'Well, *say* something,' she urged. 'Don't just sit there, making fun of me, you beast!'

'Sweetheart, take that worried look off your face. You must keep your inheritance from father. It will make him happy if you accept his gift graciously. I trust you implicitly. And as for finding anything else about you attractive or vaguely desirable, well . . .' His indifferent gaze swept her up and down, and Helen stiffened in horror until he gave a shudder of such raw, naked hunger that it made her throat constrict immediately.

'I do hope it's going to take a long time, convincing you how much I love you,' murmured Dimitri. 'Because I want to enjoy every slow, lingering second. You've entered my life with such a force that I'll never be the same again. And by the time I've finished persuading you that I love every last delicious inch of you, and that includes that sweet mind and heart of yours, then I can guarantee *you'll* never be the same again.'

Helen quivered at his tender smile. She felt her eyelids become very heavy as she lifted her face to his, and from under her closing lashes she saw and recognised the depth of his love for her.

But she didn't tell him!

His lips met hers in a kiss of searing intensity that swept away any lingering doubts, and she knew for sure that he would care for her and protect her all his life. He would smooth away any difficulties she had in moving in his world: he would welcome her father into the family and her life would be one of perfect bliss.

But still she didn't tell him!

Helen fully intended that he should spend the next few days up on the mountainside persuading her, coaxing her, courting her. And above all, loving her.

A WORLD WHERE PASSION AND DESIRE ARE FUSED

CRYSTAL FLAME — *Jayne Ann Krentz* _____ £2.95
He was fire — she was ice — together their passion was a crystal flame. An exceptional story entwining romance with the excitement of fantasy.

PINECONES AND ORCHIDS — *Suzanne Ellison* _____ £2.50
Tension and emotion lie just below the surface in this outstanding novel of love and loyalty.

BY ANY OTHER NAME — *Jeanne Triner* _____ £2.50
Money, charm, sophistication, Whitney had it all, so why return to her past? The mystery that surrounds her is revealed in this moving romance.

These three new titles will be out in bookshops from October 1988.

W❤RLDWIDE

Available from Boots, Martins, John Menzies, WH Smith, Woolworths and other paperback stockists.

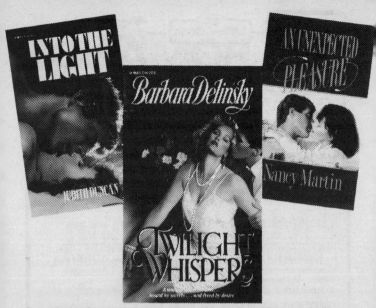

THREE TOP AUTHORS.
THREE TOP STORIES.

TWILIGHT WHISPERS — *Barbara Delinsky* — £3.50
Another superb novel from Barbara Delinsky, author of 'Within Reach' and 'Finger Prints.' This intense saga is the story of the beautiful Katia Morell, caught up in a whirlwind of power, tragedy, love and intrigue.

INTO THE LIGHT — *Judith Duncan* — £2.50
The seeds of passion sown long ago have borne bitter fruit for Natalie. Can Adam forget his resentment and forgive her for leaving, in this frank and compelling novel of emotional tension and turmoil.

AN UNEXPECTED PLEASURE — *Nancy Martin* — £2.25
A top journalist is captured by rebels in Central America and his colleague and lover follows him into the same trap. Reality blends with danger and romance in this dramatic new novel.

Available November 1988

W●RLDWIDE

Available from Boots, Martins, John Menzies, W.H. Smith, Woolworths and other paperback stockists.

ROMANCE

This Christmas Temptation Is Irresistible

Our scintillating selection makes an ideal Christmas gift. These four new novels by popular authors are only available in this gift pack. They're tempting, sensual romances created especially to satisfy the desires of today's woman and at this fantastic price you can even treat yourself!

CARDINAL RULES – *Barbara Delinsky*
A WEDDING GIFT – *Kristin James*
SUMMER WINE – *Ethel Paquin*
HOME FIRES – *Candace Schuler*

Give in to Temptation this Christmas.
Available November 1988 Price: £5.00